George A. F. H. Bradford

Letters from Portugal, Spain, Sicily and Malta

in 1812, 1813, and 1814

George A. F. H. Bradford

Letters from Portugal, Spain, Sicily and Malta
in 1812, 1813, and 1814

ISBN/EAN: 9783337291594

Printed in Europe, USA, Canada, Australia, Japan

Cover: Foto ©Andreas Hilbeck / pixelio.de

More available books at **www.hansebooks.com**

Ursula

LETTERS.

LETTERS FROM PORTUGAL,

SPAIN, SICILY, AND

MALTA,

IN 1812, 1813, AND 1814.

BY G. A. F. H. B.

LONDON:

PRIVATELY PRINTED AT THE CHISWICK PRESS.

1875.

PREFACE.

HE following letters were written by the Hon. George A. F. H. Bridgeman, afterwards Earl of Bradford, during a tour on the continent, made in company with Lord John Russell and the Hon. Robert H. Clive, in the years 1812-14.

It is thought that the notices of events during the Peninsular War give them a somewhat wider interest than is possessed by ordinary private letters, and a few copies have therefore been printed.

B.

Weston,
   May, 1875.

LETTERS.

Oporto, Thursday Evening,
August 27th, 1812.

MY DEAREST MOTHER,

OU will certainly be rather surprised to find my first letter after disembarkation dated from this place. Never to be sure were people so wonderfully fortunate as we have been to land here just at this moment. The circumstances which determined our present plans are these: I told you before I left England, I think, that we had heard a report of Lord Wellington's having defeated Marmont with immense loss. This story was corroborated from time to time on our voyage, and from four different vessels we heard that the French had lost upwards of 20,000 men, and that

B

Lord Wellington was at Madrid ; the last vessel which gave us this information was an Englishman, which we had chased for many leagues on Sunday last, thinking it was an American ; from this source we thought the report worthy of credit, as corroborating the stories we had had from Spanish and Portuguese vessels ; and John[1] and I determined (if Clive[2] should come into our wishes) to avail ourselves of the opportunity of one of the three or four merchantmen going to Oporto to carry us there, and if we found the news as good as we expected, to proceed in a short time to Madrid. On Monday morning, the 24th, we accordingly spoke the "Buzzard," and found Clive quite of our mind ; our next object was to communicate with Sir Robert Kennedy, Commissary-General of our army, who was going out to Lisbon with his wife, having been for a short time in England for his health, we thought he might perhaps be inclined to be of our party, Oporto being the nearest road to the army ; but before I proceed farther I am bound in common gratitude to express how much we were indebted to

---

[1] Lord John Russell, now Earl Russell, K.G.
[2] The Honourable Robert Henry Clive.

Captain Maitland for his great kindness to us on this, as on all other occasions. He had made us most comfortable throughout the voyage, and was indefatigable in forwarding our new schemes; it would be impossible to say too much in praise of his kindness and good nature. Sir Robert Kennedy seemed to think that he had better go on to Lisbon, as was his original intention, but he thought the news bore great marks of truth, and encouraged our plans; moreover, he was good enough (although he knew nothing of any of us) to give us a letter to Mr. McKenzie, Assistant-Commissary-General at Oporto, begging him to do all in his power to forward us. It was now mid-day, and we were abreast of the mouth of the Minho (which divides Portugal and Spain), with a fine breeze from the N.N.E.; the ships bound for Oporto were three brigs and a schooner; we found, on looking out for them, that the brigs had left the convoy in the morning without leave of the commodore, this was a blow; however, fortunately the schooner remained, and on hailing her, the master was very civil, said his accommodations were very bad, but that he would willingly take us. He was very anxious to part company; we therefore got a little cold meat as quick as possible,

and having sorted our baggage, and left all the things
we thought we could do without on board the "Pique"
(which things, together with Clive's in the "Buzzard,"
Captain Maitland promised to deposit safely at Commissioner Fraser's at Gibraltar), we proceeded on
board the "Alert" schooner with the remainder, and at
three o'clock p.m. made sail straight for Oporto, leaving the convoy to our right.   We found on board the
schooner a tidy little cabin just big enough to creep
into, and two berths in it ; we opened our cantines in
the evening, and with the help of some brown sugar
and biscuit of the master's, and our own tea, we made
a supper and a breakfast with much satisfaction.   As
usual, nothing would tempt Clive to take one of the
beds, and he laid himself down on the seat in his
cloak.   John went regularly to bed, and I laid down
on the other for a few hours, finding it much too hot
to follow John's example.   We had beautiful weather,
and our breeze kept up till after midnight, when it
became nearly calm for the rest of our voyage, and a
very thick fog came on; before daylight we were
waked by a boat full of Portuguese pilots, who came
on board and made the greatest noise I ever heard,
seeming to be in the greatest passion, but, I believe,

not being so at all, they only wanted us to give them some rum ; all went away in about a quarter of an hour, excepting one. Clive and I ran on deck to see the squabble. The fog was so thick we could not see anything of the coast; the pilot was a great treat, and could not understand or be understood except a little by John and Clive ; but I must not enter too much into particulars, or I shall never have done. After breakfast the fog cleared away a little, and we saw the shore, which was very pretty, and the low mountains which backed it were beautifully shaped. The first town we saw was Villa de Conde, three leagues north of Oporto. The only very striking thing was a very large convent of nuns towards the sea, but the view was yet very indistinct from the fog ; at eleven we came opposite Oporto Bar, the day was then beautiful, and the view of the mouth of the Douro very striking and pretty. We fancied we were arrived, but, to our disappointment, we found we must wait for a visit from the master pilot, and that the water would not be high enough to cross the Bar till two o'clock. After wasting a long time, the master pilot arrived, and told us we could not land till the following morning ; however, by

bribing the wretch with four dollars, and giving him
to understand we were people of consequence, in a
hurry to join the army, he soon changed his note, and
took us, our servants, and luggage, in his boat to
Oporto, a league above the Bar—we of course paid
well for this, but we gained our point. The river up
to Oporto is quite beautiful, but of this you have
heard. We came to an inn kept by an Englishman,
who has been here twenty-five years, and we have got
good rooms. This inn would not *quite* please you,
but it is a palace for this country. We got a good
dinner, and in the evening went with our letters to
Mr. McKenzie. We found him at supper with several
officers; he was very civil, and told us that the news
we had heard was true, but recommended our staying
a short time to hear more before we proceeded to
Madrid. This was exactly what we liked. He said
he was going the next morning before day to Lamego by land, and would return down the Douro in
boats; he was going on duty, and if he could get us
mules in time, would be glad of our company. He
immediately sent to the corregidor for mules; we
stayed late, but no answer, we went home between
eleven and twelve o'clock, and he promised to send

the mules if they came in time. Late the next morning an under-commissary came to say they could not get them, Mr. McKenzie was gone and would return in four days, and he recommended our taking a tour into the north in the meantime. We next determined to visit General Trant, governor of Oporto. He lives at present at St. Juan, a league off, at the river's mouth. We walked there, our host for our guide, and on sending up our names nothing could exceed the civility, the kindness of General Trant; he gave us the whole account of the state of military affairs, and pointed out the places on the map. Good God! how glorious is the news. He told us that the French had lost 20,000 men; that Marmont and Bonnet were desperately wounded and believed to be dead; that Lord Wellington had entered Madrid on the 12th, leaving two divisions near Valladolid to watch the wreck of the French army, which had retreated towards the Ebro, 10,000 strong, but so completely cut up, as to be considered *hors de combat;* that Joseph [1] had advanced, previous to this great battle, to join Marmont with 14,000 men, but that he had only reached

---

[1] Joseph Bonaparte, King of Spain.

Alba de Tormes when he heard of Marmont's defeat ;
that he had retreated precipitately to Madrid, and
thence, after leaving 17,000 men in the fortress of
Buen Retiro, all picked Frenchmen, he had continued
his retreat to join Suchet at Valencia ; that he had
himself very narrowly escaped, our advanced dragoons
having taken some of his own guard. The Buen
Retiro is an excessively strong place, and was expected to hold out a long time, and to have cost us a
great many lives ; however, Lord Wellington contrived
to take it by surprise on the 14th, two days after
entering Madrid. He found an immense quantity
of ordnance, stores, arms, &c. What makes all this
so very glorious and satisfactory is, that Lord Wellington was certainly in full retreat, thinking that the
enemy would be too strong for him, but suddenly
seeing the French in some confusion, he ordered an
attack just before Salamanca ; the French right endeavoured to turn our left, we refused it, and made a
most vigorous attack with our right on their left, and
totally destroyed that and their centre. They were
thunderstruck, and retreated in the utmost confusion,
followed by our victorious army, who continued to
take prisoners for many days. Our left wing was not

engaged. Thus by the success of a quarter of an hour (which decided the victory) has half Spain been freed from those accursed tyrants of the world. The sort of enthusiasm which prevails now, both in Spain and Portugal, is not to be conceived—Lord Wellington is considered almost a god. They wrote that at Madrid he can hardly pass through the streets from the crowds of men, women, and children who follow him, staring and loading him with *vivas.* It is singular that accounts state Soult to have been still before Cadiz on the 14th, although he must have known of our victory. The longer he remains there the better, as he *must* then be cut off. It is imagined he is staying there purposely, wishing to come over to the Spanish cause. Probably, my dearest mother, you will have heard everything long ago, but it is possible I may have mentioned something you have not heard. Give my duty to my grandfather,[1] and tell him I hope he will give me credit for obeying him in this respect. General Trant is a very pleasing, gentlemanly, sensible man, and, I believe, an excellent officer. His account to us was the clearest I ever heard ; he likewise showed us

---

[1] George, Fourth Viscount Torrington.

C

a plan of the battle, which had been sent to him.
Marmont's army being considered totally destroyed,
and the two divisions being left at Valladolid to watch
the remaining stragglers, it is thought that Lord
Wellington will advance into Catalonia, and join the
army which has landed at Villa Nova, to the south of
Barcelona, under General Maitland, and then march
to Valencia against Joseph and Suchet. If Soult
breaks up from Andalusia, and endeavours to form a
junction with Suchet (to which the intermediate Spanish
armies will oppose great difficulties), Hill will cross
the Tagus and join Lord Wellington. The Spaniards
are advancing from Gallicia and Asturias, and when
they reach Valladolid, will leave our two divisions at
liberty to join the Grand Army likewise. Oh! what
a bright prospect we have before us. To return to
ourselves, we were at General Trant's yesterday, and
after giving us these accounts, he offered to assist us
in any way we liked. He got several tours made out
for us, and we determined on a plan I will detail pre-
sently. He asked us to dinner; we walked down to
the river, and went thence to Oporto in a boat, and
having dressed, returned in the same way. We dined
at half-past four, and there were many officers, British

and Portuguese. We had an excellent dinner, wine and dessert in the evening. He asked several Portuguese families from San Juan to meet us—there were some pretty girls amongst them. The society is formal enough among strangers ; some danced a little, but we who were just come from England found it much too hot to join that party. During dinner (as is the Portuguese custom) several people came in, among others the prior of a large convent on the south of the Douro, opposite the town, most romantically and beautifully situated on a rock, with hanging gardens and pine woods. This prior is a pleasing young man ; he asked the Governor and his staff, and us, to dine at the convent on Friday (to-morrow), and we shall all go.

We set out on Saturday next on a tour, previous to starting finally for Madrid ; we should have gone to-morrow had it not been for the invitation to the convent ; we are going to Aveiro, Coimbra, Busaco, Vizeu, San Pedro do Sul, Arouca, Lamego, and thence down the Douro in a boat to Oporto ; this tour will take us about a week, we shall then stay two or three days here again, and after that go to Villa de Conde, Braga, Chaves, Bragança, Zamora, Toro, Valladolid,

and thence to Madrid; but you shall hear more of
this before we leave Oporto for good. General Trant
sent us three of his horses, and his town-major to accompany us this morning, and he took us a beautiful
ride, and afterwards to a convent of nuns in the
town, we saw none of the nuns, but only two Miss
Russells, who consider themselves related distantly
to the Duke of Bedford; they were delighted to see
John; the eldest is very pretty, the second promises
to be so, but is very young, they are daughters of a
Portuguese gentleman who married an English Miss
Russell; why they are called Russell I know not,
they say in Portugal people take any name they like
best; they have lost their father and mother, their aunt
is in the Brazils, and their brother in the army, and
they are put into the convent by the regency, as a
safe asylum, but are not going to take the veil. Some
time ago Major Wilde, an English officer, was a few
days in Oporto, and visited the convent, where he
saw and conversed with Miss Russell through the
grate, and the next morning he proposed to her, and
it is thought they would have been married had not
Major Wilde been obliged suddenly to quit Oporto
with the army, and he was killed, poor fellow, afterwards, at Badajoz. You would imagine the Miss

Russells spoke English, but they do not know a word of anything but Portuguese.

The English post sets off from hence every Friday evening to Lisbon, and I shall take this letter to General Trant to-morrow morning, who is so good as to send it to Mr. Stuart to forward to England. It strikes twelve, my dearest mother, and my eyes draw very long straws, my pen is worn out, and my hand tired. I hope you will have received my letters which I sent from Yarmouth, Lymington, by a Torbay boat from off Falmouth, and by the " Hope," from off Finisterre, all since we were embarked. General Trant asked us to dinner again to-day, but we excused ourselves, having so much to write and settle. God bless you, my dear mother, give my affectionate duty to my father, and love to Henry,[1] and all my relations and friends, you are with

Your ever affectionate
And dutiful son,
G. A. F. H. BRIDGEMAN.

P. S.—We heard by the " Niobe " that Admiral

---

[1] His brother, the Honourable Henry E. Bridgeman, afterwards rector of Blymhill.

Legge was coming home immediately, and Captain Cockburn appointed to succeed him. I should therefore have missed Charles,[1] and if Soult leaves Cadiz, Orlando[2] would probably follow. I am not, therefore, very sorry at not going there first, and I have seen what I wished of all things to see—viz., the north of Portugal. Clive and John desire to be very kindly remembered to you. This evening as John Cobb[3] was walking in the street, a funeral passed, and a man came up to him and offered him a lighted torch ; he was much astonished, and hurried away ; on his return home he learnt that they only wanted him to accompany the funeral.

---

[1] His brother (afterwards Admiral) the Honourable C. O. Bridgeman.

[2] His brother, the Honourable Orlando Bridgeman, Grenadier Guards, and afterwards aide-de-camp to Lord Hill at Waterloo.

[3] John Cobb, personal servant to Mr. Bridgeman, afterwards a messenger in the House of Commons.

MY DEAREST MOTHER,

E returned last night from a tour which has afforded us all much pleasure, and has on the whole been most prosperous; we followed the track I mentioned in my last written from hence about a fortnight ago, which General Trant was so good as to send through Mr. Stuart. I hope you have received it safe, as it was a long letter. Our only deviation from the above said route was, that we went from Busaco to San Pedro do Sul by a curious mountain road over the Serra de Alcoba, and through that of Cara Mula, instead of going by Vizeu, an ugly, uninteresting city; we saved very little in distance, and none in time, but we passed

through an interesting and in parts a most beautiful
country.   We saw the whole of our grand position
at Busaco, where we lodged one night at the Convent
of Carmelites Déchaussés, a small poor-looking building situated at the top of the high Serra de Busaco, in
the midst of a Quinta, which is one entire wood of
oaks, chestnuts, beautiful Portuguese cypresses, and
several sorts of evergreens.   In this warm climate it
is only on the high hills or mountain valleys that
you see oaks or, indeed, anything like fine verdure ;
the lower hills are only able to grow the pines (of
which you meet with immense forests) and the Indian
corn ; indeed, we have seen but few stubbles of our
corn, even on the high hills, and the harvest was all
in before we landed.   I will say nothing of our journey
to Coimbra, which was principally through pine woods,
except that once for a few miles we passed between
beautiful hedges of myrtle in full blossom.   This sight
struck me wonderfully, and the perfume of them was
delicious.

Coimbra is finely situated on a steep declivity of the
hills which form the north bank of the Mondego, a
river which is nearly dry in summer, leaving large
banks of sand and gravel, but in the winter is a large

river. The valley of the Mondego is very fertile. The country about Coimbra, where the hills are high and finely shaped, would be beautiful were it not that the plantations are entirely of olive, which is an ugly tree. Opposite to the city are two fine convents, and also the Quinta das Lagrimas, or Garden of Tears, famous for being the residence of poor Inez de Castro, who was there murdered by order of her father-in-law, the King of Portugal. This Quinta we visited, as also the University, where we saw a fine library, church, and museum, and a noble collection of in-struments—mathematical, &c. Hence we came to Busaco, and thence to San Pedro do Sul, where we saw the baths and springs; they are of very great heat, and contain a quantity of sulphur. In the springs women were boiling chickens. There are said to be some Roman remains in the baths, but we could find nothing of the kind. From San Pedro we went to the Bernardine Convent of San Christoval, most romantically situated in the midst of the beautiful rocky Serra de Gralieira, overhanging a rocky knoll covered with cork trees and various beautiful ever-greens, and crowned with a little chapel. This convent is very rich. There are only nine monks,

D

who received us most graciously and showed us the greatest civility and attentions. They were much better bred than the other monks we had seen in Portugal, especially the prior. We breakfasted and dined there, and departed much against their inclination, for they pressed us much to stay some days for the shooting, as there are plenty of boars, wolves, hares, and partridges. They at last allowed us to depart, with the promise of passing some days with them if we should return through Portugal. We went that night to Arouca, a village where there is the largest and richest convent of nuns in Portugal. There are seven monks belonging to it, and seventy-nine nuns. We drank tea with the nuns, and supped with the monks, who gave us rooms and beds. The next morning we breakfasted with the nuns, and we dined with the monks. We saw the church, which is quite magnificent. These people are also Bernardines. The nuns were all well bred, but the monks vulgar, eating dogs, though very civil and attentive to us. We proceeded two leagues this evening, as we could not reach Lamego in a day, and slept at such a place as never was imagined in England; here we could literally get *nothing!* fortunately we had brought a little bread with us, of which, with cold water, we made our supper and breakfast. Lamego is a dirty, old, shabby city, a league to the south of the Douro. We went hence in the morning to Regoa, the place of embarkation for Oporto, here is an English commissary; we applied to him for a boat, but we were obliged to wait at Regoa two days, and on the third (last Wednesday, the 9th,) we set off at seven, and came four leagues, which we were eight hours about, and nothing would persuade our boatmen to go any farther till yesterday morning; we had some cold meat and some wine with us, on which we dined in the boat, and slept on our mattrasses; it was an open one, but the night was very fine. Yesterday we were off at five, and at nine we reached Vimeiro, four leagues farther, and half-way between Oporto and Regoa; here we changed boats, and arrived at Oporto at nine last night. We have been at a set of curious pigsties by way of inns, and such places as we have slept in you cannot even *imagine;* our beds and clothes are full of fleas, which will be our delightful companions till we return to England; I have thousands of bites about me. We have done very well in the eating way — we have generally

managed to get starved fowls, or chickens, and eggs ;
in the towns we have had chocolate for breakfast, at
the *ventas* or inns we used our own tea and sugar ;
milk and butter are things one does not even ask for ;
in cities the wine is generally sour, but has been
drinkable, except in one or two places, when we used
our brandy, and infamous it was ; we got it here, and
it resembles whisky more than anything else; at
Regoa we got some good wine, here it is that the
port wine is made, but the *Vin du Pays*, throughout
the provinces we have been in, is a sort of port. The
Douro is a beautiful river on the whole; we came
16 leagues (or 64 miles) down it ; about Regoa and
for two leagues down, the banks, which are very
high, are entirely covered with vines, which is very
ugly, hence, the scenery was very beautiful ! the
banks were variously covered with rocks, chestnuts,
oranges, heath, pines, olives, cork trees, convents,
houses of hidalgos, and villages ; the last two leagues
to Oporto we were most unluckily in the dark, I
believe they are very beautiful. We intend staying
here till Monday, when we shall go by Braga to the
banks of the Minho, then by the Serra de Gerez to
Chaves, Bragança, Miranda de Douro, Salamanca,

and Valladolid to Madrid. I hope to find several
letters when we reach Cadiz, which will not be for
a long time; before Cadiz I see no probability of
receiving a letter. We find from the difficulty of
procuring horses and mules, that we must make another considerable diminution of our baggage, and we
intend to send George (John's servant) with these
things to Cadiz; J. Cobb and Gabriel will remain
with us, for we found there was too much for one servant to do. Our beds and one cantine are absolutely
necessary, but we shall take as few clothes as possible. I hope I shall be able to send you a letter
from Madrid, but I am not sure. I should imagine,
however, that through Sir C. Stuart it might be done.
I wish I knew him,—cannot you get Lady Stuart to
write to him about me? I have neither time nor the
means of writing to Orlando; I hope you will have
told him of the change of our plans, on receiving my
last letter, and I hope we shall meet at Cadiz some
time or other. I have been quite well since I left
you, and I think the climate will do me no harm.
Adieu, my dearest parents. Love to all.

Your ever affectionate

And dutiful son.

P.S.—General Trant's letters of recommendation were of the greatest possible use to us. The Carmelites of Busaco never eating meat, we fared most miserably there, having nothing but filthy messes of garden stuff and stinking oil; our position there seems impregnable; we followed the road thence as far as Massena's head-quarters, and saw the road by which he retreated to Sardaõ, or as it is called, Sardaon. The Falls of the Douro, of which you may have heard much, are not rapid; of all those we came down, only one was as strong as that of London Bridge.

 MUST write you a few lines, my beloved mother, to send by Friday's post, in order to give you the latest news of us from this place ; we intended to have set out yesterday, but there never was anything like the difficulty of getting horses and mules. We have bought three horses and two mules for ourselves and our servants, being unable to hire them. They are but sorry animals, but they cost us £94, or 330 dollars. General Wilson, governor of the province of Minho, whose head-quarters are at Vianna, a place on the sea-coast, 18 leagues north of Oporto, which we intend taking on our way to Madrid, is at present here, and promises to get us three baggage mules there. The

mules at this place are most of them under embargo,
for a great number of the medical staff; though I
believe there are some in the town, yet the people
deny it, thinking that if they were to let us take them
to Madrid they would be taken for the army. We
are going to-day to try every possible means of getting
three to go as far as Vianna, and if we succeed we
shall start to-morrow. We intend going to Gui-
maraens and Braga, Ponte de Lima, Vianna, and Ca-
minha, at the mouth of the Minho, thence up the river
to Valença, and back to Ponte de Lima and Braga ;
from Braga we shall go to Montalegre, seeing the
bridge of Salamonde (over which Soult made his
famous retreat after his defeat at Oporto), and the
Serra de Gerez, that lofty range which separates the
province of Minho from Galicia ; then to Chaves,
Bragança, Miranda de Douro, and Salamanca ; here
we shall have the pleasure of viewing the field of
battle where our army covered themselves with eternal
glory, and we shall pursue the retreat of the French
by Alba de Tormes and Tordesillas, to Valladolid ;
thence taking the great road through Arevalo and
the Pass of Guadarrama to Madrid. This journey will
probably take us six weeks to perform, which will

bring us to the end of October. I suppose we shall reach Cadiz towards the close of the year. By the bye, after writing my last letter to you on the 11th, we heard of Soult having broken up from Seville and Cadiz. I hope if the Guards quit the latter place in consequence of this, that I shall be fortunate enough to meet with Orlando somewhere. I think, my dear mother, that through Sir C. Stuart you might contrive to send me one letter to Madrid, as we shall certainly be there as late as two months from this time. There never was anything equal to the civility we have met with from everybody here. Marshal Beresford and his staff arrived on Friday from Salamanca, where he has been since he received his wounds; he embarked yesterday for Lisbon; he is wonderfully well considering the severity of his wounds. His arrival here made the place very gay: the first night all the rank and fashion (as we say in England), attended him at the play, where there were several flowery *eulogia* addressed to him from the stage. It is a very pretty little theatre, but not sufficiently lighted. The performance was a tragic comedy, and a ballet; the former I was not a judge of, but I believe it was bad; the ballet was intolerable.

E

The boxes are nearly all private, and the style of thing resembles our opera, the men going about from box to box. Saturday we had a ball, given by the Senhor Susa Mollo; Sunday, another by Senhora Pamplona; and yesterday a third at the English Factory House, where the rooms are very handsome. At the first I was made to dance with a lady who could only speak Portuguese; yesterday and the day before I got partners who could talk English. I am the only gay one of our trio; Clive and John have danced from necessity, but very little. Friday we dined at home; Saturday with Marshal Beresford; Sunday with Mr. Croft to meet the Marshal; and yesterday at General Trant's, who is now living in the city, but will return soon to San Juan. A man has just been here from the governor, who gives us great hopes of procuring mules; we shall know in two or three hours' time. We find money go very fast here: we have made acquaintance with an English wine merchant, Mr. Hinde, who has changed £200 English notes which I had, and has advanced £300 to Clive, which I hope will see us to Madrid; but this horse buying and feeding is expensive work, and we English always get well cheated by foreigners. It is lucky we met with Mr. Hinde, for our letters of credit do not avail us here; we are told they will be accepted at Madrid. I wanted to learn a little Spanish, but would you believe it, there is not a Spanish grammar or Spanish book of any description to be bought in this great Cidada do Porto, the second of the kingdom. Clive has lent me a Spanish dictionary, and I shall purchase a grammar and some easy books at Salamanca. I shall very soon be able to read it—but the pronunciation is the Devil. Adieu for the present,

My dearest Mother.

 HAVE only five minutes, my dear mother, to tell you that we bought three mules yesterday. Two of them are very fine ones, the third moderate; we were obliged to pay $510, which is £153, for them. We are now going to pay our farewell visit to General Trant, and we shall then proceed to a village four leagues off, half-way between this place and Guimaraens. Clive desires to be kindly remembered to you, and that I will say he intends writing to you from Madrid. George (John's servant) does not go with us, he stays here to get some of our things washed, and then proceeds with all our extra luggage in a transport, or a merchant vessel, to Lisbon, and thence to Cadiz. Clive will not let me add another word. God bless my dear parents and friends.

Your ever affectionate, &c., &c.

MY DEAREST MOTHER,

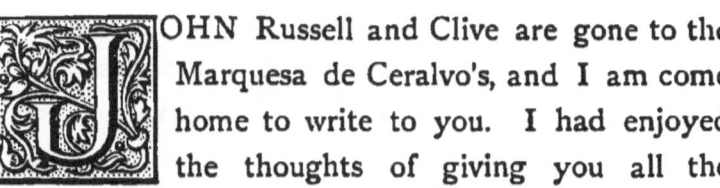

OHN Russell and Clive are gone to the Marquesa de Ceralvo's, and I am come home to write to you. I had enjoyed the thoughts of giving you all the correct information I have collected touching our army, sick, &c., but my companions tell me that were I to specify numbers, my letter would probably be stopped before it reached you. Now, this is so extraordinary to me, and so unlike anything British, that I cannot believe it; nevertheless, as they tell me so who from experience ought to know, I shall follow their advice, as I would rather that you should hear little than nothing from me. I just added my duty to a few lines John sent to you from Bragança, which

I hope you will get ; we then thought to arrive here in four days, but found the distance was twenty-five instead of nineteen leagues, which took us five days. We had quitted the beautiful country on coming into the province of Traz os Montes from that of Minho, which latter is extremely fine. Traz os Montes is a track of rugged, barren mountains ; the cities of Chaves and of Bragança are wretched places. Braga, Guimarães, and the other towns of the Minho, are handsome, rich, and beautifully situated ; and the Serra de Gerez, through a great part of which we passed, between Braga and Chaves, is very grand. On entering Spain at Villariño, a large village at the mouth of the River Tormes, I was much struck with the difference of dress, which is, in Spain, exceedingly ornamental, especially the women's, who wear a great variety of colours and embroidery, with their hair tied in a knot behind with different coloured ribbons. I have not had much time yet to judge of the people of Spain, but they appear, if civilly treated (for they require the greatest civility to be paid to them), to be amiable and obliging, and their manners very graceful and captivating. From Villariño we came by Ledesma to this place. We have had beautiful

weather ever since we landed, until the 6th (the day
of our arrival here), during which it rained torrents;
the succeeding days have been much colder than
is usual at this season in England, and, to-day excepted, with long heavy showers. We had letters to
Dr. Curtis and the Marques de Ceralvo here—the
former rector of the Irish College, and an agreeable,
intelligent man, who has been of great use to our
army; the other is a young grandee; they have both
been very civil to us, as well as everybody else we
have met. Yesterday we dined with the Marques,
and to-day with the Purveyor-General Dixon. We
have seen most of the remains of the beautiful buildings here; it is enough to drive one distracted to see
the devastation committed by the French barbarity—
cursed vipers! who destroy but for the sake of destruction. The cathedral, as to building, remains
entire, and is altogether a grand and beautiful fabric,
but the architecture is very far from pure. There
were here twenty-five colleges, and as many convents:
seventeen of the former, and about eleven of the
latter, are totally destroyed, and the rest turned into
barracks or hospitals. The sort of hatred which a
spectator must feel towards the destroyers is not to

be conceived.   The College del Rey and the Convent
of San Vicente are the two which the French employed so much labour to make into fortresses ; these
were thought but little of in England, and people
imagined they were to be taken in an instant.   We
went over the remains of them, and their strength
must have been immense ; the French employed
1,000 workmen at them for near three years.   We
went to-day to the immortal field of Arapiles, it is a
sad sight, however, for the ground is still covered
with unburied carcasses of men and horses, on which
flocks of vultures were feeding ; the stench even at
this distant period of above eleven weeks, is very
great ; and those who were there some time ago
during the hot weather, described it as *dreadful.* We
followed the enemy so fast that we had not time to
bury half the dead, and the Spaniards are much too
idle and slothful to stir themselves for their noble
and generous allies ; they are a strange mixture of
nobleness, sloth, and want of feeling.   We have not
heard of the taking of the Castle of Burgos yet, but
it has probably fallen ere this, and the news is expected to arrive here to-morrow.   We start in the
morning for Valladolid, and talk of going thence to

Burgos, and afterwards by Segovia to Madrid, where it is supposed Lord Wellington will go as soon as Burgos falls.

El Rey Jose is said to be at Saragossa; Suchet and Soult united in Valencia; Marmont and Bonnet are gone to France, the former will not allow his arm to be amputated, they are both said to be for ever *hors de combat.* Hill is at Madrid. God bless you my dear parents, &c. Soult is said to have 75,000 men, Clausel 30,000, but very much scattered for provisions. Hill 4,000 at Madrid, Lord Wellington I know not. We have a great many sick here, and this sudden cold has carried off several.

VALLADOLID,
October 16th, 1812.

MY DEAREST MOTHER,

 HAVE only time to write you a very few lines to say that we got here on the 14th, saw this curious and large old town yesterday, and are just on the point of setting out for Burgos; the castle there makes an obstinate resistance, and has already cost us many lives, it is uncommonly strong, and the garrison 2,000 men. On the 13th the French attacked our advanced posts beyond Burgos, and Colonel Ponsonby was wounded severely in the thigh by a musket-ball; however, the ball was immediately extracted, and has not injured the bone, so that he is likely, I am happy to say, to do well. We go to Burgos with only J. Cobb, and two or three changes of linen

and our blankets, and we shall return here on our way to Madrid, for we can get no information as to the direct road from Burgos by the Pass of Somo-sierra.

One of our finest mules has been lamed in shoeing, and we were forced to leave him with our second muleteer at a village between Salamanca and this place, and hire one to come on. God knows when our own will be well. We have a report from head-quarters of the total defeat of the Russians, with the loss of 40,000 men, and the entry of the French into Moscow. I trust this is untrue, or I fear all will be over. We have had rainy weather for the last ten days, an unfortunate thing for our poor fellows at Burgos! As we approach nearer to the seat of war melancholy sights present themselves. Yesterday we saw several bullock-carts with wounded men coming in, and it is shocking to see the torture they suffer by being jolted over the stones. If the slothful Spaniards had one grain of humanity or generosity, they would meet these poor fellows at the entrance of the towns and carry them over the stones ; but no ! they hate the French, and receive us everywhere with loud acclamations, and then forsooth return to their

former indolent habits, hoping and expecting everything must go on as they wish, but preferring to be
conquered to making the slightest exertion in their
own defence.   I have only time to offer you my most
affectionate duty, and to send my kind love to all
those who care for me.

Your ever dutiful son, &c. &c.

I hear the third battalion of the First Guards are
coming or come to Madrid, where I hope I shall meet
Orlando.

MY DEAREST FATHER,

WE left this place a month ago in order to enjoy the consequences of the glorious battle of Arapiles, and we have returned here in haste after having been witnesses to two precipitate retreats. Never surely was there a greater disappointment to us English and Spaniards! Nor is it at all impossible that the army may very soon return to Portugal; perhaps before this letter reaches you.

Our whole army is now united near Arevalo, the head-quarters at Buedo; and there are several Spanish armies with us under Castaños, perhaps 30,000. Our army, British and Portuguese, may be about 40,000 effectives. The bridges over the Douro are all blown up, excepting at Toro, which the French have got possession of, and they have crossed over three regiments of infantry to form a *tête du pont*, and some cavalry, who a day or two back, advanced to Alaijos, about three or four leagues towards the south-east. Marmont's old army, now under General Souham, are stretched along the north bank of the Douro, and are supposed to amount to 40,000, some say to 48,000! but this I don't believe. Soult has advanced from the south with all the men he could collect of his own, Suchet's, and Joseph's armies, having evacuated Valencia entirely, and he is supposed to have at least 60,000 men. But he has left in his rear our army under Mackenzie (formerly Maitland's) and three Spanish armies, under Ballesteros, O'Donnell, and Roche, but where they are, or what they are about, we have not even a guess. Such, my dear father, are the reports of this place, as we have been able to collect them, and I have given them to you, although you probably know in England a thousand times better than we do here, but I think you may like to know the reports from all quarters. Lord Wellington having been appointed Generalissimo of the Spanish armies is a great thing, but it is ·melancholy to see the slow progress with which the new levies proceed ; there have, as yet, only been 150 recruits raised in the immense province of Castille, although the whole country swarms with men ready to enter the army at a moment's notice. The Spaniards are a fine people and deserve to be free, but their government and the higher orders are despicable ; their hatred for the French exceeds anything I could have imagined, and their minds can never be conquered by them. Some time or other their cause must succeed, but I fear years have yet to roll away ere that glorious end can be accomplished ; but if it pleases God that I should live to a moderate age, I do not despair of seeing the overbearing Corsican crushed to atoms by the united and persevering efforts of England and Spain.

I will now give you a short account of our last month's tour, or rather three weeks', for I fancy it is about that time since I wrote from Valladolid. We got as far as head-quarters at Villatoro, near Burgos, and stayed there one day. We rode to see our posi- tion in front, and saw the French descend in large columns, apparently to attack us. We gave way a little, when Lord Wellington brought down the First Division, upon which the French immediately retired

without engaging. This was considered a recon-
noitring, and everyone was prepared for a battle the
next day, and the head-quarters were removed farther
in front. In the morning we sent our baggage and J.
Cobb into Burgos, meaning to sleep there that night
(for although the town is immediately under the castle,
the inhabitants could not be hurt without their de-
stroying the town, and this they would not do), and
we rode again to the front. We remained there some
hours, but the French did not show any disposition to
attack, and all idea of a battle that day being given
up, we were returning to Burgos when we heard that
news had arrived from the south which determined
Lord Wellington immediately to retire over the Douro.
This was a blow to us! We entered Burgos, found
our baggage, dined, and proceeded three leagues on
our return to a small village, where all we could get
was an uninhabited roof and a little straw. The next
morning the French entered Burgos. We stopped
one day in Valladolid, and proceeded by Arivalo to
Segovia. But I have forgot Burgos. It is a fine town,
and the cathedral quite beautiful; the castle is immense, and strength itself. It contained a garrison of
two thousand men, and cost us at least that number in

the siege. We arrived at Segovia on the 30th ult. It is a fine old city, and the situation of it magnificent. The castle stands beautifully, and is a venerable old pile, especially the old Torre, famous as the prison of Gil Blas. The cathedral is very handsome, and contains a great deal of fine painted glass—the Spanish cathedrals have been famous for fine pictures, but the French have got them all. The next day we went to San Ildefonso, a magnificent and beautifully situated palace at the foot of the Guadalaxara ; the gardens are very fine, and laid out in the old taste, with magnificent water-works, which do not now play ; we were lodged in the palace, which is very comfortable, and beautifully furnished. There is an extensive collection of pictures, and it appeared to us to contain numbers of fine ones, but we wanted light to see them ; there are also some fine statues and marbles. While looking over these a peasant arrived, and told us the French were in Madrid, and the allies in full retreat. We got off early the next morning, and entered the great road to Corunna, by which our army retreated by San Rafael. Here we found ourselves in the midst of our retreating army, which confirmed the peasant's report, and left us nothing but to make the

G

best of our way to Salamanca, cruelly disappointed at
having been cut off from seeing Madrid and the Escurial. Here we had some more hardships, for Clive
having stayed behind for our baggage while John and I
went on to procure a night's lodging, we missed each
other, and did not join again for four and twenty
hours, during which John and I got neither beds nor
a single mouthful to eat; however, we were in high
luck to join again the next morning. One thing that
I lament among many others is, that I know not now
when I shall be able to learn the Spanish language,
which it is impossible to do while in constant motion,
and I had intended to have had a master at Madrid.
Henry Williams was here yesterday, on his way from
Cadiz to England, and he brought me letters from
Charles and Orlando. Alas! poor Orlando is cruelly
disappointed at being kept at Isla; I hope he will
soon remove, poor fellow! but I fear he is very unwell.
Charles will probably be in England ere this reaches
you. Pray give him my kind love, and a thousand
thanks for his letter. I wish he had stayed a little
longer at Cadiz, and we should then have met there;
possibly something may bring him into this part of
the world before I leave it, but the chance is small, I

fear. Their letters were dated the 4th and 5th of October. Orlando says he is to be moved to Lisbon when he is better; if I could be certain of finding him there, I would contrive to take it in my way to Cadiz; but as it is so uncertain, and that nothing will persuade John and Clive to go there, I believe I had better give up all thoughts of it. I had fancied myself very near Orlando when in the midst of Hill's army, until I got his letter yesterday. We intend to go from hence to Cadiz, taking in our way Ciudad Rodrigo, Alcantara, Badajoz, Merida, and Seville, and if it is safe, also Cordova, Andujar, Jaen, Granada, Malaga, and Gibraltar. I begged of my mother, in a letter from Oporto, to write to me at Madrid; if she was so good as to do so, I fear the letter must be lost, but who would have imagined it at the time I wrote! We have had generally fine weather lately, and for two or three hours in the afternoon the sun has been scorching, but the rest of the twenty-four hours the cold has been astonishing, far exceeding that of England, and the want of fire-places in this country is most severely felt by us. We are liable in this town to a surprise from the French crossing at Toro; but we have 1,500 convalescents as a garrison, and there is a Moorish wall round the town, at all the gates of which we have sentries, and two cavalry piquets are posted on different roads, two leagues off, to give the alarm, so that if they send any small detachments I think they will get the worst of it. We intend remaining here a few days unless Lord Wellington should retire further—we arrived the day before yesterday. We have never got our mule that we left behind us lame ; we have heard of its following us to Segovia, but I fear either the French, English, or Spaniards have got possession of her ; she is a beautiful creature, and a great loss. We have bought another at Valladolid, but he does not turn out very well. Accept, my dear parents, my kind relations and friends, my united and sincere love, affection, and duty,

And believe me, &c. &c.

BADAJOZ,
November 23rd, 1812.

MY DEAR MOTHER,

INCE my last we have travelled over a large tract of country, most of it devoid of interest, and very ugly. Spain is indeed, I believe, altogether as ugly a country as the globe contains; however, there are some fine scenes in passing through the Sierra de Gata, which divides Leon and Estremadura. Ciudad Rodrigo is a nasty old town, and half of it a heap of ruins. Its situation is naturally strong, but the walls old and crazy; the breach which was made in the last siege, and which the Spaniards had rebuilt, has fallen down again, and they are once more employed in slowly replacing it. Alcantara possesses a work well worth travelling many leagues to see. I mean

its magnificent Roman bridge over the Tagus, which here runs in a deep and narrow bed of bare and almost perpendicular rocks. The parapet of the bridge when we were there was 115 feet above the water, and in summer is more. The span of the centre arch is 107 feet, and of the other two principal ones (of which one is blown up) 90 feet. It has three other smaller arches, built on the rocky banks. The road over it is a perfect flat. I know not if I mentioned the Roman aqueduct we saw at Segovia; that is, without any exception, the most beautiful and grandest edifice I ever beheld. The parapet is 102 feet high; but it would be in vain for me to attempt a description of it—I only wish you could see it. Elvas is very prettily situated, and surrounded by very finely shaped hills covered with olives. Fort la Lippe crowns the highest of them, and it is as beautiful an object as it is a strong fort. Badajoz is in a frightful country, of which itself is no great ornament. The garrison consists of near 5,000 Spaniards, and the governor's name is Rodriguez. The Marques de Palacios (Governor-General of Estremadura) is resident here, but they say is on the point of being removed, why, I do not hear. Ballesteros, they say,

is a prisoner at Gibraltar, having kicked at Lord
Wellington's appointment as Generalissimo, and he
has written several violent letters to the Regency;
where his army is, or by whom commanded, we
cannot learn. We have heard reports of our army,
which are bad; but we know nothing for certain.
They say Suchet remains very strong in Valencia;
that Lord William Bentinck has taken the command
of our army at Alicante, bringing 5,000 fresh troops,
but is not able to cope with him. Lord Wellington,
they say, has retired to Rodrigo with much loss,
particularly in cavalry; that the French have 11,000
cavalry in the field; that we have totally lost the 16th
Light Dragoons and a regiment of Dragoon Guards;
besides which, that a German regiment of cavalry has
been dreadfully cut up. The whole of this may be
false, and the greatest part probably is. I tell you
the reports we get at each place as I think they may
amuse you, but they are not to be depended upon.
At some town on our road (I think Albuquerque) this
affair of cavalry was made out to be a great victory on
our side, and a total overthrow of the French cavalry.
The sanguine disposition and absurd credulity of the
lower class of Spaniards are beyond conception.

Since we left Leon and Castille and entered Estremadura we have found a great difference in the people. The former are amiable, of pleasing manners, obliging, and speak the purest Castillian; the Estremeños are sulky, of rough manners, disobliging, and their language scarcely intelligible. However, they all seem equally to detest the French, but they are by no means as grateful to us! In this town it is not surprising, for I fear it is a melancholy truth, that the horrid and unnatural enormities committed by our soldiery after the assault, were before almost unheard of. We have, on the whole, been fortunate in our weather, having had few thorough rainy days. We arrived here on Saturday, and are staying to get our linen washed. We hope to get away about Thursday, for this is a nasty place, and we have got a miserable billet. Clive has been writing to you this morning. We are all (masters and servants) very prosperous. The latter detest this country, and will have fine stories to tell in the servants' hall about it. We go from hence to Merida, thence to Seville. I have written to Colonel Capel to beg of him to send me a line to Seville to inform me whether Orlando is still at Isla, or gone to Lisbon; if the former we shall proceed immediately to Cadiz, if the latter we shall first visit Cordova and Granada; in the former case we shall be at Cadiz in eighteen or nineteen days, and I hope there to have a little news from England, after an ignorance of between four and five months. We went round the ramparts yesterday, and it quite staggers me to see the walls our men climbed to take the castle; the ladders were not high enough, and when they were full of men others below lifted them up, ladders and all. This end of the town and that washed by the Guadiana excepted, the walls are by no means strong, and the great strength consists in the three outworks:—San Christoval, Pardaleras, and Picuriña. We are going to see them to-day.

God bless you, &c. &c.

H

MY DEAREST MOTHER,

 TAKE up my pen with particular pleasure here, as this letter will give you information of several things which will be agreeable to you, I am sure. I have to acknowledge several letters from England, which have given me more comfort than I can express, although the pleasure I have had in reading them was damped by the very indifferent accounts they contain of my much valued grandfather; but I will no longer delay to tell you that I found Orlando still here, a great piece of good fortune. I cannot say he is quite recovered, but I trust in a few days more he will be so; he intends to write to you by the next packet, and will tell you our mutual proceedings

here. I will therefore confine myself to what we have done since I last wrote, and our future plans, as far as I can, but these are unsettled. We were pleased with Merida, which is a nice old town, and contains most extensive remains of the Romans, two aqueducts, an amphitheatre, and a naumachia, with temples, and houses in ruins; a fine triumphal arch, and a bridge without an end, I really never could count the arches of it ; it is partly Roman, repaired successively by the Moors and Spaniards ; hence to Seville the road was uninteresting. Seville is a most magnificent and a most delightful town, and one can never see enough of the cathedral ; there are a vast number of public buildings, many of which are very handsome palaces. The climate, the moment we came to the south of the Sierra Morena, was most extraordinary ; all to the north is very little warmer than England, but the four days we were at Seville were actually like the month of August with us; the thermometer was 71° in the shade, and the evenings and nights quite sultry. Seville is very remarkable for the beauty of its women, but I fear they bestow all their charms on the French, and sigh for their return ; they dress quite beautifully, and the Paséo (walk) or Alaméda was crowded with them on Sunday evening, and the gayest, prettiest scene I ever beheld. Seville is a most curious town for any one to see who never was before in Andalucia, of which it is the radiant queen; its streets are almost all extremely narrow, but the houses are very large, and quite delightful; they have one or two large courts, to which the rooms or corridors open. These courts are paved with different coloured tiles, and ornamented by fountains and orange trees, and several have small marble pillars. The staircases, and around the doors, are also marble; the floors are generally of coloured tiles, and floors of wood are scarcely ever seen in Spain—never in the south—they are commonly of bricks. This description of a house is nearly applicable to all this southern country, but in the greatest perfection at Seville. I saw the Funçion in the cathedral there on the Fiesta de la Concepcion, and I cannot say how disappointed I was, having heard so much of the magnificence of such fiestas in Spain, and especially in Seville Cathedral, which is one of the richest churches in Spain. The exterior of it is an unfinished pile of mixed architecture, but is immense, and, altogether, has a grand appearance. There is a very

high tower, the greatest part Moorish, which you
ascend without steps—it is called the Girálda (in
Spanish pronunciation Hirálda), and from the top of
it there is a magnificent view of the city and its
environs. The country is not pretty, but the hills are
covered with olives planted in rows, and present a
lively and cultivated appearance ; and the gardens of
vegetables round the town are well cultivated. The
orange gardens belonging to the palace, and the convents with myrtle hedges, are delightful. At Xeres,
on our way here, we called on M. Gordon, a sherry
merchant, whom John knew, and he gave us some of
the best sherry I ever tasted. I wish there was a butt
of it at Weston. Xeres is a very pretty town, and
Puerto de Santa Maria, and Cadiz, are beautiful. Isla
is a large, good town ; but poor Puerto Real is entirely
destroyed by the French. John and Clive came
straight here ; I stayed at Isla for a day with Orlando,
and we then came here together ; we and John have
got a good lodging upon the Bay, and close to the
Alaméda ; Clive is at Sir H. Wellesley's—we came
here on the 15th. I am going to work hard at
Spanish, and hope to have a master to-morrow. I
have picked up a good deal of the language from my

grammar, and talking with the peasants, and I can read it tolerably with occasional assistance from the dictionary; but I want a master, and some good society, very much. Lord Wellington has been expected for the last two days, and Sir Henry is at Santa Maria waiting for him. I hope his coming will make this place very gay. We have altered our plans in consequence of hearing that the fever is over in Murcia; we now intend to stay here three weeks longer, and then we shall go to Gibraltar, Malaga, and Granada, thence to Cordova, and back to Granada, whence we shall proceed to Murcia, Cartagena, and Alicante, and there embark for Port Mahon, from whence we are sure of a passage to Malta or to Sicily. It is singular that we shall have been through so very large a part of the Peninsula without seeing either of the capitals; we were cruelly out of luck about Madrid. I have laid out about £60 in books here; I hope they will get safe to England. Clive says I may send them to Sir H. Wellesley's, to go with some of his from thence. I have got a large folio of the maps of Spain, by Lopez, the best there are, and I shall endeavour wherever I go to procure the best maps I can of each country, for they are delightful things to

have. Our mules and horses are all well, and have
served us most famously. Things in the Peninsula
have not a very bright face at present; they report
that the French are advancing through Estremadura
towards Seville, and Lord Wellington's delay seems
to strengthen it, as he might be forced to take a cir-
cuitous route, and come by Agramonte. They talk
much of an insurrection; these Andaluses are a bad
people; the Sevillians want to change the government, and set up the old Seville Junta again; Cordova
and Jaen are said to have joined them, and they
offered Castaños the Regency. He has discovered
the plan, and the heads are taken up and brought
here. They say the people here are discontented, but
I don't think anything will come from this. The
Andaluses are a poor, paltry set; you would have
been astonished to have seen the peasants at Arapiles
ploughing their lands in the midst of the putrid carcasses; but you can have no idea of the inertness of
these people, without seeing it. They were employed
in their fields with the greatest *sang froid* in this
pestilential air. They have no notion of doing one
iota more than appears to them absolutely necessary
for the moment. There is a good play-house here,

and some good actors and Bolero dancers. I have seen all the Spanish and gipsy dances, and most curious and singular they are—the Fandango is pretty; the Spanish Contra Dansa is very pretty too; the time is the same as the waltz, and there is a great deal of waltzing in them, which, introduced in figures, is beautiful. I long to dance them, but I cannot speak Spanish well enough to be at my ease. We have had terribly rainy weather ever since we were at Seville until yesterday, since when it has been fine, but rather sharp; we feel the want of fires. Sir Henry Wellesley has famous ones, and his house is very comfortable.

December 23rd.—Still no intelligence of Lord Wellington. There is a debate this morning in the Cortes on the subject of these Seville delinquents; Clive and John are going to hear it, but I am not forward enough in the language to understand it—it is expected to be very animated. There is no order yet for the packet's sailing, and I suppose she will be detained till the Duque's arrival—I mean Lord Wellington. I shall keep my letter open till the last moment, though I shall probably have little to say. I have seen Charles's friends, the Villa Vicencias and

Boronis, but the nicest girl I have seen is the daughter of the Duquesa de Goa; she is very young, but has a pretty face and figure, dances beautifully, and has pretty manners, which is more than can be said of all the Spanish girls, who are terribly vulgar and forward.

December 28th.—I have nothing, my dear mother, to say to-day. Orlando has mentioned Lord Wellington's arrival, he is gone to-day to see the Spanish and British troops at the Isla. It is a most wretched day—violent storms of wind and rain. Two balls are to be given to Lord Wellington, one by Sir Henry Wellesley, which they say is to be the day after to-morrow; and the other by the grandees who are here, the day for which is not yet fixed. We shall dine at home, as Sir Henry has a very large party of merchants and officers. Lord Wellington dined with the Regency on Saturday, and afterwards went to the theatre, where he was well received; the house was illuminated, and patriotic songs were sung. They have put Spanish words to our " God save the King," introducing George the Third and Ferdinando the Seventh together. " George " in Spanish is a frightful word, it is spelt " Jorge " and pronounced " Horky."

I

There are a swarm of English travellers expected here from Lisbon, they are on the road, and may arrive any day, to the number of twenty. I fancy Sir Henry is a little annoyed at the idea, as it has always been his custom to give general invitations to all English travellers. We had a pleasant dinner enough yesterday at Costello's. There was a dance at the theatre the other night that I had not seen before—the Seguidillas Manchegas (à la Mancha Danse), which is excessively pretty. The number of different national Spanish dances is very great, almost every province has one peculiar to itself, they are all danced with castanets, and in the most beautiful dresses. There are several good dancers of these dances at the theatre, but sometimes they attempt short French ballets, and they make sad work of them; we go every night to the play. I wish you could know the language, it is as beautiful as the Italian, and grandeur itself. On Monday the performance was entirely by women, a singular, but, of course, a tiresome thing; there was a comedy, a short musical piece, boleros, a little French ballet, and a farce, and all the parts were played by women; even the prompter was a woman! and they managed the scenery, trimmed the lamps, in short, did everything, and would not allow a man to approach behind the scenes; they really got through it wonderfully well, though they were a little tedious.   Yesterday Orlando dined with General Cooke, and John and I with Sir Henry, who gave a grand dinner to the Regency and big-wigs; there were above forty persons, and the table was very handsome.   We went afterwards to some theatricals at la Señora Orgullo's; she has made a pretty little theatre of one of her rooms, and they performed a comedy, an opera, and boleros; there was a cousin of the lady's (a girl only fourteen years old) who acted excessively well in the comedy, and Señora Orgullo and two gentlemen sung very well in the opera.   To-day Lord Wellington went to the Cortes, where he made them a speech of thanks, and had an answer from the President as empty of essence as it was full of flummery and vanity; they both read their speeches.   Lord Wellington was much applauded from the gallery; but there is a large French party here, who take great pains to insinuate that we are going to betray Spain, take the government into our own hands, and declare Lord Wellington regent; this is generally supposed the cause of his not having been received on landing with any applause, and of the little that he has since met with ; he dines to-day with Mr. Duff, the British Consul, as do the embassy and the general and his staff, we again, therefore, dine at home. The ambassador's ball takes place to-night. We had torrents of rain all yesterday, to-day it is dry but cloudy.

January 1st, 1813.—A merry Christmas and a happy New Year to you all, my dear parents and friends ; the packet sails to-day, and I shall take my letters after breakfast to Clive. Sir Henry's ball was very handsome, and there were crowds of people ; six hundred were invited, but not near that number came. Our departure is not fixed, but it will probably be in about ten days. Lord Wellington is expected to go in three or four. Lord Herbert,[1] with a crowd of travellers, is at Seville, waiting, I understand, for a bull feast which is appointed for the 6th, but probably will not take place so soon. I get on a little with my Spanish, and I venture to talk sometimes to the ladies. God bless you, &c., &c.

---

[1] The late Earl of Pembroke.

CADIZ,
January 22nd, 1813.

MY DEAREST MOTHER,

EDNESDAY morning two packets came in from England, bringing me your letters 13, 14, and 15, which I have been long anxiously expecting. We had been without a packet from England ever since the 17th of December; I had learnt the death of my poor grand-father [1] from Clive, who saw it in the "Courier" of the 17th ult., which had come overland from Lisbon about a fortnight ago; it did not surprise me at all, as I had been expecting the event some time from the melancholy accounts I had previously received of him from you, but you will easily conceive how anxious I have ever since been to learn the melan-

---

[1] Viscount Torrington.

choly particulars of his last days and those that succeeded his death; that it was easy and without any
pain is a comfortable reflection, and as, alas! all en-
joyment of this life seemed for some time to have
left him, an easy relief from its cares and infirmities
was a thing rather to be desired than lamented. Yet,
my dear mother, that he should have been deprived
in his last moments, dear amiable old man, of the
power of expressing all his wishes, must, I fear, have
caused him considerable mental suffering, and the
account of this distressed me greatly. However, I
am much to blame in writing thus to you, my dearest
mother, who, Heaven knows, will have sufficient grief
of your own without being worried with other people's
feelings on this melancholy subject. You know how
much I loved my dear kind grandfather, who always
behaved with such true affection to me; and although
when I took leave of him I felt convinced it was for
the last time, yet the certainty that one never is again
to behold in this world a beloved and highly-valued
parent and friend cannot be heard unmoved.

Pardon me, my dear mother, the pain this may give
you; I am sure you would have been hurt had I been
quite silent on the subject—which once entered upon,

the pen will sometimes follow the feelings further
than it should.   You will probably have heard from
Orlando from Lisbon; he sailed from hence on the
evening of the 8th instant, with Captain Bateman in
the "Stately," for that port.   I have not heard of his
arrival, and I fear he must have had a bad voyage,
for the wind has been very adverse; he was fortunate
to get so good a passage; we have been waiting here
some time longer than we intended for the arrival of
the packet; we shall now start on Monday next, the
25th, sleep that night at Isla, and get to Gibraltar on
the Thursday; we intend to go over from thence to
Ceuta and Tetuan, and to stay a few days at the
latter place for shooting.   We shall not remain many
days at Gibraltar, but proceed, as I mentioned in my
last letter, to Alicante, there to embark for Malta.   I
am much disappointed at the fall of a plan that was
in agitation for a short time; when Lord Wellington
was here he was constantly talking of being early in
the summer at Madrid, and several times advised
John to stay for the opening of the next campaign;
John and Clive in consequence proposed this to me,
which I came into with delight; I intended to have
gone from hence after seeing Gibraltar and Granada,

to Lisbon, and we were all to have followed the army to Madrid, if open. Why or wherefore I know not (for they give no reason), the two originators of the plan are now obstinately and immoveably against it, and I foresee now that I shall never see Lisbon or Madrid.

It is probable that we shall return to England by Russia or France (for I think by that time we are likely to be at peace). Herbert arrived here some time ago with several Englishmen from Lisbon; he brought me a letter from old Bromley,[1] which was very gratifying. Herbert will join us in Sicily, and accompany us in our eastern tour. Upon second thoughts I determined to purchase a pipe of sherry for my father while I was on the spot; I have got it from M. Costello, from whom Clive has purchased four for different persons, of the same sort; it appears to us to be excellent wine, and I hope it will prove so; I have paid for the wine and freightage, and nothing remains to be paid but the disembarkation and duty. Tell Lucy,[2] with my love, that I have

---

[1] One of the Harrow masters, and tutor to Mr. Bridgeman.

[2] His sister, afterwards Lady Lucy Whitmore, wife of W. Wolryche Whitmore, Esq., M.P.

taken the greatest pains to procure her some Spanish music, but hitherto without success. Music is not printed in this country, and the only means of having it is to get it copied; this my friend Ysnardi promised to do for me; he spoke to a music-master, and if it is not finished before I go he promises to send it to you. There is to be the Fandango, the Seguidillas Manchegas, some Boleros, Cachuchas, and Oles, and the Zapateado—all dances, the last, of the Gypsies; there are also some songs and a march: the Spanish music is pretty, very peculiar and characteristic. I fear Lucy will find it difficult to catch the style and time unless she meets with somebody who has been in Spain. I have been unlucky about my Spanish master. He is in the Commissariat Office, and this made him so irregular in coming to me that I gave him up. I only got fourteen lessons of an hour each. My books, with Clive's and John's, we intend sending to Gibraltar, and there we hope Commissioner Fraser will get some King's ship to take them to England. We have seen all the fortifications and defences of this island; they are immensely strong and extensive. I believe it is the strongest place by nature and art in the world. They say it is

K

much stronger than Gibraltar. Its great strength
consists in the marshy lands and salt ditches with
which it is surrounded on the land side, rendering it
impossible for troops to approach it in large bodies.
They are cutting a canal across the Trocadero to the
river San Pedro, which will insulate the part nearest
to Cadiz. This is an immense work, and though a
thousand workmen are employed upon it, it will not
be completed for many months. I certainly was
guilty of a great error if I did not mention having
seen Lord Wellington at Burgos. We dined with
him at 9 o'clock the day we passed at head-quarters,
after having seen the advance of the French—surely I
must have mentioned our misfortune in not seeing
them driven back that evening. This it was which
made Lord Wellington so late back at head-quarters.
He had very few of his aides-de-camp there with
him. I liked much what I saw of the Prince of
Orange; he seems a fine, manly, young fellow, and
bears an excellent character. When we proceeded
from Burgos to Madrid we were aware that it was
likely soon to be given up, but we determined to try
if we could not get there just in time to see it—we
knew it depended on the celerity of Soult. Surely I

mentioned that Clive and the baggage passed us while we were looking out for them, on the road close to the village where John and I passed the night. They proceeded to Villa Castin—the town we had originally determined to stop at. The night being very dark caused us to miss seeing them among the crowds of baggage, mules, carts, troops, &c. &c., and the excessive confusion of the scene. They passed us about eight o'clock, and John and I continued keeping watch alternately on the road till ten. The night was pitch dark and piercing cold, with a damp fog falling, and we were nearly in a torpid state. We started from our hovel very early, and reached Villà Castin at daybreak, where, in the market-place, we were inexpressibly delighted to find Clive and J. Cobb looking out for us. The reason we had stopped at the other village was that we knew great numbers of troops were to put up at Villa Castin, and we thought every roof would be occupied. As it was, in neither place could we be said to have found shelter, either for man or beast.

January 23rd.—There are accounts from Alicante which mention indications of general movements in the French armies of Valencia, &c., &c. It is here

confidently believed that they intend making an attack
on Alicante or retiring over the Ebro; the latter
opinion is the most prevalent. The ball given by the
grandees to Lord Wellington on the 4th was very
magnificent, but the crowds were so immense that
people could not stir; nothing that I ever saw in
London can be compared to it. They say it cost
near 20,000 dollars. The supper tables and other
decorations were handsome and in good taste, but so
little good order was preserved that people of all
descriptions got in, and the tables were filled four or
five different times. There were covers only for 300,
and it is calculated that near 3,000 were present at
the same time. There were several good devices both
in Latin and Spanish, and the united flags of Great
Britain, Russia, and Portugal in all directions. The
heat was precisely that of a hot-house, but of course
of a more disagreeable nature; nevertheless the
Spanish women were not deterred from dancing, or
rather jostling in the crowd. I left about thirty or
forty couples dancing at half-past seven, and it continued till nine. There was a great display of beauty
and of magnificent dresses. The grand supper-table
was a beautiful sight when first filled. It contained

120 covers, which were all occupied by ladies, excepting Lord Wellington, his brother, and three or four other men. There was a malicious report that Lord Wellington was to be poisoned, and the ladies would not allow him, poor hungry man, to touch anything. The Duchess of Osuna sent for some dishes from her own house for him. Sir Henry Wellesley gave a second ball on the 9th, which I was not at, having just heard the news of my poor grandfather's death. Lord Wellington went the following day through Badajoz to Lisbon. John's servant (who, by the way, is an excellent one) came here from Oporto, *viâ* Lisbon. Fortunately a transport is going hence to Gibraltar on Tuesday, in which he will go with our heavy luggage; thence we intend to send him on to Malta. You need not think about our want of comforts, for I know not why, but travellers do not feel those things as might be expected, and they are much greater in imagination than in fact. A great friend of mine is now here, Lord Bayning. He will go to the Isla with us on Monday and proceed as far as the field of Barrosa, whence he will return here.

God bless you, my dearest mother, &c., &c.

GIBRALTAR,
February 2nd, 1813.

MY DEAR MOTHER,

HE packet is to sail for England to-morrow, therefore I will write to you the little I have to say since leaving Cadiz. John and I went to the Isla on Monday the 25th, but Clive could not get our passports till Wednesday, on which day he joined us with them early in the morning, and we proceeded over the Barrosa field of battle, still strewed with carcases, to Vejer, a curious old town, situated at the summit of a steep, rocky hill, six leagues from Isla. John, who had bought a gun at Cadiz, dawdled behind on the Barrosa hills in search of game, while Clive and I regularly proceeded on. Four leagues from Isla we came to the small town of Conil, on the sea cliffs.

From hence the road to Vejer, two leagues, is quite shocking—road, indeed, it could not be called, it was merely the tracks of footsteps over fields. The soil is a tenacious clay, in which the animals sunk each step nearly knee deep ; we were obliged to walk, and were one plaster of clay to the knees. We passed a river, and it soon after became pitch dark. Thus we proceeded for some time, and at last came up to our servants and mules, the latter having, three of them, fallen, from being quite unable to keep their feet in the clay. We passed them, and soon after lost our way, and got into boggy rivers. Fortunately, in the silence of the night we heard the muleteers speaking to the mules, halloed to them, and soon joined them. Once more all together, we pursued our way to Vejer, where we arrived at nine o'clock ; at twelve we quite gave up poor John, and went to bed. The following day at twelve he appeared, and told us that he had proceeded half a league beyond Conil the preceding night, when losing his way he determined to return to Conil. He passed the river prosperously, but on the other side, just as he was going to rise the hill (being most fortunately himself on foot), his pony sunk up to its neck in a quicksand. He in vain endeavoured to help

him out, and went to the town for assistance. Having
procured two men and two boys, they with difficulty
got the poor helpless animal out. John got a little
bread 'and a bed, and joined us, as I have already
stated, the following day. We found that Tarifa was
seven leagues from Vejer, and that there was no place
whatever between, and they told us the roads were
still worse than those we had come. We therefore
remained Thursday at Vejer, and replaced the shoes
our poor beasts had lost in the clay. Friday, as soon
as it was light, we started, and fortunately arrived at
Tarifa at half-past six, an hour after dark. We found
the road horrible in places, but not all the way ; on
the whole I reckon this one of the most extraordinary
day's journeys we have performed. Tarifa is a poor
place, and nothing but the abominable rainy weather
could have saved it from the French. It is nearly six
leagues from hence, and the road dreadful ; we therefore only came half-way (to Algeciras) the next day,
and reached this place on Sunday, the 31st, at one
o'clock, being the seventh day since we left Cadiz.
The country from Vejer to Gibraltar is beautiful. The
rocky mountains, covered with magnificent cork trees,
and abounding in streams, have a very grand effect.

I believe I forgot to tell you that Commissioner Fraser had invited us to be with them when we came to Gibraltar. Here, then, John and I are comfortably established in one of the prettiest country houses you ever saw, and enjoying all the luxuries of England with the southern climate. Clive is at the Lieutenant-Governor's, where we all dine to-day. This house is situated a mile south of the town, high up on the Rock, and in the midst of a delightful garden full of violets and geraniums; the trees are already all budding, and will soon afford shade. I am as much pleased with Gibraltar Bay as I was disappointed with that of Cadiz. This is surrounded with fine mountains, and the African coast is very bold. The Rock itself is most beautiful and curious—it is 1,000 feet high. I have seen the Galleries and some other things, but I have yet much to see. We are going over, in a day or two, to Ceuta and Tetuan. Captain Godby, General Campbell's aide-de-camp, who has dogs, and knows the country at Tetuan, will go with us, and, perhaps, the Commissioner, in whose yacht we are to go. I will write again before we leave this place for the last of Spain.

God bless you, &c. &c.

L

E have remained here thus long in hopes of the easterly wind changing, and enabling us to go to Tetuan, but it is obstinate. The Commissioner and Captain Godby were going with us, but it is not possible to land at Tetuan with an easterly wind, on account of the surf upon the Bar; we now have determined, John, Clive, and I, to go over to Ceuta to-morrow in the Commissioner's yacht, and he and Captain Godby will take us up there on Friday, should the wind be favourable, if not, he will send his yacht to bring us back, I shall be very sorry to miss Tetuan, both on account of the shooting and of seeing a Moorish town; the Moors do not allow anybody to enter their territories from Ceuta, which prevents our going from

thence by land. There never was anything so delightful as the weather; the first blossoms are beautiful, and everything has the appearance of spring
—this is the finest season here—in summer the heat
is insufferable, it is now as hot as the greater part of
our summer, and the nights are delightful; I hope
the rainy season is almost over. We saw a great deal
of Sir Montague and Lady Burgoyne here, and I like
them very much; he is rather fussy, but very good-
humoured. Still fine news from Russia! We have
received the "Gazettes" of the 17th and 20th January; but this letter of Lord Wellington's to the commanding officers of regiments is rather unpleasant. I
grieve that the army has shown such a total want of
discipline. Poor Tyrconnell! how truly grieved I am
to hear of his death—he was a fine fellow! We intend going by Ronda to Malaga, it is three or four
leagues round, but it is worth seeing—it is a large
town, situated on a high mountain. The Sierra de
Ronda is one of the finest ranges of mountains in
Spain, and is said to contain some magnificent scenery. The highest and finest mountains of all are
those of the Sierra Nevada, or Snowy Mountains, to
the south-east of Granada—they are higher than the

Pyrenees. What a curious scene this place presents from the number of different nations one sees in the streets! There are English, Spaniards, Moors, Portuguese, Italians, Genoese, Algerians, Greeks, and Jews; I hear that Malta is much more extraordinary in this respect.

Wednesday, the 10*th.*—The wind is still east, my dearest mother, and we are just embarking for Ceuta, where we shall probably be landed in three hours' time. I am writing this from the Commissioner's Office in the dock yard, while waiting for Clive—he is just arrived.

God bless you, &c., &c.

GIBRALTAR,
February 26th, 1813.

MY DEAREST MOTHER,

HE three inclosed sheets are addressed to William Childe,[1] but as I think parts of them may be interesting to you, especially that which relates to our Barbary excursion, I have sent them open that you may read them, after which pray forward them to him. We found Wrottesley in the "Sabine," lying in Ceuta Bay ; we slept while at Ceuta at a tolerable inn, and lived with General Fraser, who commands the troops there. Ceuta is a most singular peninsula, with a delightful bay, and excellent anchorage for boats and shipping ; if ever we are at war with Spain again, it

---

[1] The present W. Lacon Childe, Esq., of Kinlet, Shropshire.

will be a very desirable thing for us to take, as it is far preferable to Gibraltar, and the two together would completely command the Straits. We remained two nights at Ceuta, and the wind not changing we returned to Gibraltar with Wrottesley. The next day, Saturday, the 13th, the wind came round to the westward, and the Commissioner, Captain Godby, and ourselves, went over to Tetuan in the " Sabine." Wrottesley remained on shore with us, and we had a very jolly party, but not good sport. We got a miserable room in the Custom House, two miles up the river and four from the town. The mountains here are very magnificent; they are part of Mount Atlas, which extends hundreds of miles up the country; we lived very well, Captain Godby's sergeant being a good cook; we got meat, bread, &c., from the town, and drinkables we took with us. We had one room only for ourselves and another for our servants; we had just space in ours to sling three cots and to put our three beds under them; they were all obliged to be taken down before we could put a table for our breakfast. Wrottesley brought the Commissioner and me home on Friday, and we landed on Saturday morning; the other three were obliged to wait for a

passport till Sunday ; the two naval officers did not
require one, and I (being rather unwell and not able
to shoot again) contrived to smuggle myself on
board.   We go from hence to-morrow.

God bless you, &c., &c.

Inclosed in the above.

Here we are; nearly seven months after leaving England, although when we sailed, on the 4th of August, we
imagined we were coming immediately to this place.
You will have heard from my mother of our having
quitted the fleet off the coast of Portugal, and gone
in a merchant schooner to Oporto, where we dis-
embarked on the 25th of August, after a tiresome
long passage of three weeks ; since this we have
travelled a great number of leagues in the Peninsula,
and seen a great deal of the people in all situations.
The Spanish peasantry and the minor gentry, who are
not placemen, are a *very* fine people ; the former
(were it not for a lamentable indolence which reigns
throughout Spain to a most incredible degree) would
in my opinion be the finest people in the universe ;

the grandees are not near so bad as by many they
have been represented; five-sixths of them have
followed the patriotic party, and have borne their
poverty and deprivations with wonderful patience and
fortitude. Of those few who have followed El Rey
Pepe (as they mockingly call Joseph here) most of
them have been compelled by force, and would be delighted to escape the first opportunity; many did
escape to Cadiz on the late hasty evacuation of the
capital by Joseph. They have all for generations been
kept in a state of ignorance and want of common
education almost incredible, by the cursed government
which this poor country has so long suffered under;
this will naturally cause all their actions to be weak,
and weakness appears to me their greatest fault.
Now I come to the worst class of Spaniards—the
placemen—these are to the last degree despicable.
From the lowest wretches in the municipalities to the
heads of the government almost, there is scarcely a
mean act under the sun that they will not perform to
put a dollar into their pockets. The Portuguese are
a kind hospitable people, but most despicably servile,
and the greatest cheats and thieves in the world, and
will do anything for a bribe; their peasantry have

not one grain of that beautiful nobleness of character
and strict honour which is so striking in that of
Spain; nor are the manners of the upper orders in
Portugal to be mentioned with those of Spain. The
dress of the Spanish ladies is characteristic and
beautiful, that of the Portuguese frightful, being bad
imitations of the most vulgar English dresses; there
are vast numbers of rather pretty women in Spain,
but I don't think I have seen above two or three very
pretty, and certainly not one beautiful; they have
excessively pretty figures, beautiful feet, and a most
graceful carriage, they are good - humoured, great
coquettes, quick, and lively, but without a grain of
modesty or of fine feeling; they are pleasant companions to a passing traveller, but I never saw one for
whom I could feel the slightest interest. The dress
of the peasantry in many parts of Spain is peculiar,
ornamental, gay, and pretty; in Portugal the women
are generally ugly, and the dress of all classes frightful; the manners, too, of the ladies are very vulgar
and disagreeable—they have not the liveliness, quickness, nor grace of the Spanish. The Portuguese
language, owing to their pronunciation, is frightful;
the Spanish, beautiful. The Spanish men are some-

M

times agreeable, but they have not the liveliness or good-nature of the ladies. The greater part of the time we have been in the Peninsula we have been moving about, but we were ten days in Oporto, and six weeks at Cadiz, where we saw all the society there is; indeed, we were very fortunate, for while we were at the former place, Maréchal Beresford arrived there, the greatest man in Portugal; and while at Cadiz we had Lord Wellington, one of the greatest in Spain; there is very little society, and that little is dull. There is a pretty theatre at Cadiz, and a tolerable set of actors; I went every night to the play, and I was delighted with the national dances, of which they have several; they say that in good times there is excellent society in Madrid, and a great deal of gaiety and magnificence. Alas! poor people, the latter is now totally out of their reach, and for the former they have but little inclination. The army and navy abuse the poor Spaniards without mercy, and would give up the cause; but I can faithfully say that from the observations I have been able to make (and I have travelled over a great deal of Spain, and lived among all classes of people), I am fully persuaded they are inveterate enemies to

the French, to whom they will *never* tamely bow, and
that they are as grateful and attached to us as their
native pride and jealousy will allow them ; moreover,
that if ever they are fortunate enough to fall under a
good government, they will make all the exertions we
can wish. The hearts of the people are firm and immut-
able ; they have borne severe and most trying hardships without complaint, and will continue to do so,
and they are ready to serve their country in any way
they may be ordered ; but a great machine cannot
move without wheels, and they have no government
that can or will organize them. You probably know
of our ill-luck in not being able to reach Madrid. We
met Hill's army on its retreat when within nine leagues
(thirty-six miles) of that place ; with this exception
we have been fortunate, and have seen a great deal.
We are just returned from Africa, where we have been
on a shooting party at Tetuan. The country is excessively wild, and the walking very severe, and a
great part of it up to the knees in marshes. I got
rather too much of it, and was a little unwell for two
or three days, but I am quite well again. There are a
great many partridges there ; they are red-legged, but
larger and more beautiful than the French. We were

too late in the season, and had not very good sport;
the weather is much like our fine September weather,
but the sun more scorching. The Moors are a strange
set of savages; they have both a contempt and a
hatred for Christians which is surprising; but they
like the English much better than any others—some
few of them are really fond of us: they abhor the
French and Spaniards. You cannot stir without a
Moorish soldier, for they shoot at you through their
rush hedges. Tetuan is a large town, and capital of a
province, but a mean, dirty place, and totally without
regularity. There are seven hundred Jews there, who
live in a separate quarter of the town. The manner
in which the Moors treat these poor exiles is perfectly
shocking—the meanest Moorish boy may murder them
with impunity; and a Jew dare not even frown at one
of them. The Moorish women may not be seen if
they walk out; their faces, all but their eyes, are
covered. The Jewesses are, some of them, very
pretty; their dress is much ornamented, but unbe-
coming. The dress of the Moors of both sexes is very
simple, generally a single garment of white linen,
which covers the head and all in the men, and comes
nearly to the knees; they have short drawers of the

same, yellow or red slippers, and no stockings. The women's garments come rather below the knee, and they wear a frightful flapping straw hat. The situation of this place, *i. e.* Gibraltar, is very beautiful—the Bay, the Rock, and opposite mountains of Barbary, far exceed my expectations. The town of Gibraltar is bad and ugly; the fortifications, particularly the galleries in the Rock, are beautiful, but the latter appear most absurd and useless; it is impossible the soldiers should ever bear the smoke and noise of firing them. We have seen some beautiful scenery in the north of Portugal. It is a very romantic, mountainous country, and the Spanish chestnuts there are quite magnificent—they exceed even our finest oak woods in size and beauty. It abounds also in arbutus, the finest heath, ten feet high, and *some* fine oaks, a great deal of rocky scenery, and the finest, clearest mountain rivers. The valleys are uncommonly rich in the province of Minho, covered with Indian corn. The number of streams preserve a constant coolness and verdure. South of the Douro the country is much more arid, and the mountain scenery is sometimes excessively grand. I have not seen Lisbon and its environs, which I lament very much, but my companions willed otherwise. The greater part of what I have seen of Spain is an ugly, uninteresting country, and most tiresome to travel over—there are immense parched plains, without a single bush to break the view. We appear now to have got into a prettier country, but there is no freshness—the finest trees they have are the corks, and they are very sombre. Seville is a fine city, full of handsome public buildings, but the French have destroyed numbers of them; the cathedral, supposed to be the finest in the world, is uninjured. I never saw anything so beautiful as the interior—it is immensely large; I could spend half my life in admiring it. There are some beautiful pictures, but the finest in Seville were in a convent, painted by Murillo—these the French have robbed it of. Salamanca is one of the most melancholy examples of French barbarity you can well imagine. The French have never injured any of the cathedrals further than taking away the fine pictures; that of Salamanca is therefore unhurt, and is a fine building; but of twenty-four colleges and the same number of convents, seventeen colleges and about a dozen convents are levelled, and the remainder bare walls without roofs, excepting two or three convents of nuns.

These buildings were all of stone, and of very fine ornamented architecture. Salamanca must have been
one of the most beautiful towns in the world—it is
now a melancholy heap of ruins. Burgos is a fine
town. The cathedral is very beautiful; it is the
second finest in Spain. It is infinitely smaller than
that at Seville, but the exterior is much more beautiful.
There are many interesting Roman remains in this
country. The aqueduct at Segovia, which is still perfect, and supplies the city, is the most beautiful work
I ever beheld ; that, and the bridge of Alcantara, exceed all I could have imagined ; the latter is built over
the Tagus, where it rolls its full waters over rocks in
a deep, narrow bed ; the banks are bare rocks, and
nearly perpendicular to an astonishing height. We
are just going to resume our journey. We go to
Malaga and Granada, thence to Cordova, and afterwards through Murcia to Cartagena and Alicante ;
there (unless Lord Wellington will open some more of
Spain to us) we shall embark for Sicily.

GRANADA,
April 14th, 1813.

MY DEAREST MOTHER,

LIVE intends sending a letter home from hence, through the embassy at Cadiz, and this will go with his. John, I believe, wrote a few lines from hence last month. He has now left us, and we two have returned here without him. But I will go regularly through our proceedings since we left Malaga, where I wrote you a letter through Commissioner Fraser, which I hope you will have received.[1] We left Malaga on the 7th of March, and came straight here by Velez, Malaga, and Alhama. We remained here about a week, during which we were much surprised at the weather;

---

[1] This letter has not yet reached me.—L. E. B.

for the day after our arrival we had a great deal of snow, and the cold continued excessive for the whole week. All the smaller streams were stopped and completely frozen up, and as we had no fireplaces or glass windows, I never suffered from cold so much in my life. This weather, you may imagine, astonished us not a little in this southern latitude, but it proceeds from the vicinity of Granada to the Sierra Nevada (or Snowy Sierra) mountains, so very high that they are covered with perpetual snow. The winters here are, in consequence, very severe, but the months of May and June quite heavenly—the country is beautiful, especially in those months. The town is very large, and situated on the sides of low hills at the north-west foot of the Sierra, and to the west there is a fine plain, watered by the river Genal, and irrigated, so that it is a perfect garden of riches. It is called the Vega (or large field) of Granada, and is encompassed on all sides with mountains of different heights and shapes. The Alhambra (the famous Moorish palace here) is quite beautiful. The exterior of this palace is miserable, but the moment you enter the gate the workmanship of the pillars, arches, floors, walls, and ceilings of the courts and apartments exceeds in

N

minuteness and delicacy all that I could have
imagined. It is the prettiest enchanting sight I ever
saw, but has no pretensions to magnificence; it is
much too finical and minute for that. The court
which is so famous and so much admired, called the
Court of the Lions, is quite small, but contains nearly
one hundred and fifty marble pillars. A stream of
water, with fountains, runs the length of it, and in the
centre is a large basin of white marble, of one single
piece, supported by twelve strange animals intended
for lions. The style of this palace and its singular
beauties are by me quite indescribable, being unlike
anything else I know; but the incalculable time and
labour they must have taken is wonderful. Charles
the Fifth did a great deal to this palace to preserve it,
and he also began one in the Grecian architecture
close to it, which would, if finished, have been quite
beautiful; but he did not even complete the masonry
of it *entirely.* It is by far the prettiest Grecian architecture I ever saw. The exterior is square and the
court circular, having a cloister supported by a regular
colonnade of thirty-two marble pillars of the Ionic
order, and a corridor above with the same number
in the Composite order. The doorways and other

parts of the building are of different marbles, and
the rest of fine stone, beautifully worked. There
are also many basso-relievos of battles on marble.
There is a convent, a priory, and several other buildings on the same hill with the palace, covering altogether a considerable extent, and the whole surrounded with a regular Moorish wall. The whole
enclosure is called the Alhambra, and is a very
striking feature from the town and its environs.
The cathedral of Granada is a very fine Grecian
building, and though much ill-treated with the gilding
and daubing of the good Catholics of this bigoted
country, yet it has many specimens of marbles, and
some tolerable sculptures and pictures, to boast of,
and altogether has a grand and venerable appearance :
connected with it, and of much older date, is the
Royal Chapel, a fine old Gothic building, erected by
King Ferdinand the Catholic, on taking this city from
the Moors. It contains two magnificent tombs, of the
most beautiful sculpture I ever beheld, and entirely
of white marble ; one is the tomb of Ferdinand and
Isabella, the Catholics, and the other of Philip the
First and Joanna. We were treated in Granada with
very great civility, and one of the ladies to whom we

brought letters gave us a ball. We went from hence on the 17th, and reached Cordova on the 20th ; it is a large but ill-built town, in a beautifully rich country. We were fortunate enough to stay there on a Sunday, and we went to the Paseo (public walk), which is the prettiest I ever saw. The weather was heavenly (for as soon as we had got a few leagues from Granada we left the cold behind us), and this walk being situated between the town and the foot of the Sierra Morena, and crowded with beautiful women most beautifully dressed, and the surrounding country being a perfect garden, I hardly ever witnessed so gay a scene. The cathedral at Cordova is exceedingly curious, being an immense Moorish mosque, containing nearly six hundred pillars, mostly of marble. This is the only mosque left in Spain, and they have built a choir and altar in the centre of bad Gothic, which, being high, and the rest of the building *very* low and square, added to the multitude of tawdry gilded chapels peeping under the Moorish horse-shoe arches, altogether has the most singular appearance imaginable ; this mosque is very large, but not handsome. From Cordova we went on the great Madrid road by Andujar, Baylen, Carolina, and Santa Cruz,

as far as Valdepeñas in La Mancha. We had then
great hopes of reaching Madrid, but the French in
small parties still continued to watch the Tagus, and
we determined to go to Almaden (about seventy or
eighty miles to our westward), in order to pass a little
time. Almaden is situated near the north of the
Sierra Morena, immediately above Cordova, and is
famous for its quicksilver mines—except one in Germany and one in South America, I fancy these of the
Sierra Morena are the only known ones in the world,
and that of Almaden is much the largest and richest of
any. We descended nearly three hundred yards into
it by perpendicular ladders, and with lamps, and a
most curious sight it was. There are four other mines
in different parts of this Sierra, but this of Almaden
is the only one at present worked. It was known in
the time of the Romans, and is mentioned slightly by
Pliny. It used to send annually to Cadiz (to be
shipped for America, to work the silver mines there),
from twenty to twenty-four thousand quintals (or
hundredweights) of pure quicksilver. The mine is
calculated to be worth 80,000,000 of reals annually, which, reckoning four dollars to the pound,
equals 1,000,000 sterling; the annual expenses to be

subtracted were 1,500,000 reals. Spain has also a contract for the produce of the Hungary mine, which produces 12,000 quintals annually. This is shipped in Trieste, and likewise sent to America. Only think of the indolence of this nation—preferring to purchase quicksilver from Austria to working their other, or rather one or two of their other smaller mines. The ore contains sulphur and quicksilver, and the richest (of which they have a great quantity) contains three parts out of four of the latter. It is a beautiful vermilion colour, and the paint is made by a very simple process —the pure quicksilver is reimpregnated with sulphur, which reduces it to a hard stone, this is ground to a fine powder, which is the vermilion paint. The quicksilver itself is extracted from the ore very simply in ovens, and with a very inconsiderable heat the sulphur evaporates, and the quicksilver fuses and rises to the top of the oven and runs off into large clay tubes, where it is retained till it cools ; for were it to be exposed to the air while warm, such is its volatility, that much would escape and be lost. I know not if this account will be at all interesting to you, my dear mother, but I have written it as it may be so to some-

body, my kind friend Mr. Chap.,[1] for instance, to whom
I always would be most kindly remembered.   The ore
is not found in veins, but in what they term *bancos*,
or banks.   *These* are *irregular* veins, not running
straight, and the same bank varying in width from
two to fifteen yards.   They almost always lie ob-
liquely, ascending to the east and descending to the
west.   The ore is likewise found in immense solid, un-
connected blocks of fifteen or twenty yards' diameter.
I have said more about this quicksilver mine on
account of the rarity of them.   This is Government
property; and although, as you may imagine, it is
destruction in a very short time to the constitutions
of these poor miners, yet they are miserably paid.
Nevertheless they never have a want of workmen.
Mineralogy brings into my head good Mr. Dickenson.[2]
I hope he enjoys the same health and even spirits
which his regular habits and benevolent mind so
justly merit; give him my kindest remembrance when
you see him.   After seeing the mine of Almaden, and

---

[1] The Rev. Mr. Chappelow, private chaplain to Lord Bradford.
[2] The Rev. Mr. Dickenson, author of a work on the " Natural
History of Staffordshire."

finding the French did not continue their retreat, John Russell, my strange cousin, and your ladyship's mad nephew, determined to execute a plan which he had often threatened, but it appeared to Clive and me so very injudicious a one that we never had an idea of his putting it into execution. However, the evening previous to our leaving Almaden, he said, " Well, I shall go to the army to see William,[1] and I will meet you either at Madrid or Alicante." We found he was quite serious, and he then informed us of his intentions. He said he should stay the next day at Almaden to sell his pony and buy something bigger. He would not take his servant, but ordered him to leave out half-a-dozen changes of linen, and his gun loaded. He was dressed in a blue great-coat, overalls and boots, a cocked hat, and sword; and literally took nothing else except his dressing-case, a pair of pantaloons and shoes, a journal and an account-book, pens and ink, and a bag of money. He would not carry anything to reload his gun, which he said his principal reason for taking was to sell, should he

---

[1] Lord George William Russell, aide-de-camp to the Duke of Wellington.

be short of money (for we had too little to spare him any). The next morning he sold his pony, bought a young horse, and rode the first league with us. Here we parted with each other with real regret, and poor John seemed to feel rather forlorn. God grant he may have reached head-quarters in safety and health, for he had been far from well the last few days he was with us. He returned to Almaden, there to purchase some leathern bags to carry his clothes, and he was to start the following morning. Clive and I feel fully persuaded that we shall see him no more till we return to England. We came back to this place by Cordova; our road from Almaden to Cordova was about seventy miles, and entirely through the Sierra Morena. This Sierra is a most singular range of mountains. It is not high in any part, nor ever retains snow upon it; but it is of immense extent, being one perfectly unbroken range from the borders of the kingdom of Murcia to those of Portugal on the Guadiana, and great part of it one hundred miles in breadth. Our road through it, from Almaden, was nothing but the track of beasts of burthen, and for thirty or forty miles it lay through the wildest mountains you can imagine, and a constant ascent or descent in this dis-

o

tance. We passed one poor village, where we slept, and, except this, it was a perfect desert, where here and there we met a few donkeys laden. Some parts were covered only with low shrubs, so common in this country, the rest was a pine forest ; but when we arrived on the southern ridge of the Sierra, I never beheld so magnificent, so enchanting a scene. Ourselves still in this forest of pines, we beheld Cordova in its golden valley immediately below us, and surrounded by kitchen gardens, olive grounds, convents, and country houses. Beyond the river, hills covered with green corn, and in the distance, to the southwest, the mountains towards Granada and Jaen topped with snow ; had but these corn-hills had our hedgerows, nothing would have been wanting. We descended from the Sierra by rugged winding paths in this pine forest, the ground covered with shrubs, the laurustinus in profusion and in full bloom, and the whole extent enamelled with cistus—there were four sorts in bloom, three white, and the fourth a beautiful purple. Notwithstanding the great length of time it took us to descend, I never felt more regret in my life than on reaching the bottom, and leaving behind me this enchanting garden of nature. I think (and sin-

cerely hope) the picture of it will ever be before my
eyes in its liveliest colours. We reached this place
for the second time last Sunday, the 11th, and we are
staying here to rest our animals and see the Easter
gaieties. About Wednesday we shall start for Cartagena, where we shall pass two or three days, and
then proceed by Murcia to Alicante, always providing
that the moment the French are good enough to
evacuate Madrid, we take the direct road there. If,
on reaching Alicante, Madrid is still occupied by the
enemy, we shall embark for Minorca and Sicily.
Some bad news arrived here yesterday from the east,
but they seem to know no particulars; the wise news-
mongers are looking very black, and rather insinuate
against our Alicante army. All I can learn is, that
part of our army has been surprised and cut off by a
corps of 8,000 from Suchet's—this General Murray
did *not* prevent; whether he *could* have done so, or
could not, remains to be proved—Elio should take care
of his own, and not Murray. On our return here we
found the air still sharp and keen, but since the change
of the moon on Thursday, it has been very hot; the
summer is now setting in, and in the plains of Murcia
we shall be fried alive.

April 20th.—Clive wished not to send his letter till to-day, that he might write word to his friends at Cadiz the event of the elections of deputies for this kingdom to the new Cortes, which is appointed to meet in October next ; the kingdom of Granada sends ten.   I cannot inform you whether the event has been satisfactory or no to the patriots in this particular instance, but I grieve to say that, speaking generally of Spain, the clergy are making immense efforts, and have gained great power again over the minds of the weak and *beatos* (or devotees), and there is much reason to fear that if they can obtain many votes, they will re-establish that dreadful tribunal of the Inquisition.   If they should succeed, this poor unhappy country, after all it has already suffered, must unavoidably experience the scenes of a bloody revolution ; for the body of the nation abhor the Inquisition, and as it has once been abolished, they will never tamely submit to its re-establishment.   We leave this place to-morrow for Cartagena.

&c. &c.

ALICANTE,
May 12th, 1813.

MY DEAREST MOTHER,

 HAVE several letters to thank you for, and to acknowledge. . . . .
Since I wrote to you from Granada we have seen little that has been interesting ; the country thence to the entrance of the kingdom of Murcia is dreary and miserable. Lorca and Cartagena have fine olive and corn plains—the latter has a nice little bay, and the naval arsenal is very handsome, compact, and commodious ; at present it is quite deserted. Murcia itself is a fine town, and has a cathedral altogether handsome, but very irregular in architecture ; the huerta (or garden) of Murcia, as it is called, which is an irrigated valley of from twenty to thirty miles long from west to east, and perhaps

ten broad, sheltered to the north and south by two
rows of low mountains, is the richest spot of ground,
perhaps, in the universe, certainly in the Peninsula ;
the greater part is corn, the crops of which exceeded
in luxuriance anything I ever beheld.   Amongst the
corn, mulberry trees are thickly planted, beneath
whose shade the corn was quite as fine as where exposed to the sun ; the rest is planted with orange trees,
whence all this part of Spain is supplied with the fruit.
The fragrance of their flowers scented the whole
atmosphere ; the barley was ripe, and some of it cut,
and the wheat nearly ripe.   Lucern grows here in the
greatest profusion, and yields a crop nearly every
month of the year.   Grass of all sorts grows here most
luxuriantly, which seems very strange in this burning
climate, but it must be owing to the irrigation and to
the shade afforded by the mulberry trees.   Immense
quantities of silk is made here, and in the town there
is a royal manufactory.   This valley continues with
the same luxuriance of production eastward towards
the sea, and there it is called the Huerta de Orihuela,
but how far that extends I know not.   Alicante is a
vile, detestable place ; the people of the kingdom of
Valencia are the worst in Spain—they are an ill-

affected, selfish, grumbling race ; their language is an
ugly mixture of French and old Spanish, though they
understand the Castilian ; they are very sulky, and
unaccommodating to the English, by whom, in return,
they are detested.   Our army here seems to be full of
misunderstandings and party, but I cannot dive into
the truth ; one party blames General Murray violently
for not having followed up the repulse of the French
at Castalla, whom they say we might have destroyed.
The hot weather seems to have set in, and exercise
begins to be rather oppressive, except in the mornings
and evenings.   The mosquitos begin to swarm, and
the first night I arrived, sleeping without a mos-
quito net, I was so bit round the eyes, that the
swelling made me half blind ; but the net completely keeps them off ; by the bye, I fancied
mosquitos a great deal larger than our gnat, but I
find they are the identical same, only that there are
more of them, and the bite is sharper in these
hot climates ; that of the common fly here is dreadfully sharp, and as they crawl (which the mosquitos
do not) no net can keep them off.   I think I mentioned in Oporto how much the flies worried us there.
I don't think I have yet mentioned the day of our

arrival here, which was the 7th; our animals all
lasted out the journey; though of the horses my
little tough mountaineer alone remains uninjured, the
other three are all quite done for; the mules are all
sound but one, which has a splint and swelled leg
from work; however, from the excessive low price of
animals here, through fear of embargo, we are only to
get $250 for these four mules, which cost us $630. I
get $15 for my pony, which cost me $60. Clive has
given his away; and the servants' horses may fetch
$20 together. I wish you could see my pony, he is a
bay, about 12 hands high, $5\frac{1}{2}$ feet long, with a mane
reaching half way to the ground, his tail is docked
by the Portigooses (otherwise Portuguese) in supposed
imitation of the English. The numbers of people
now in this wretched town (owing to numbers having
entered for safety from the French, and others from a
large suburb which was pulled down for the sake of
defence), in addition to the army, is something astonishing, and there is no getting a room anywhere;
I am in a miserable one at the house of our Consul,
Mr. Attey, the dirt of which, and of his family
(Spanish) exceeds all I ever beheld, but he is very
kind and civil, and thinks it all perfection. Clive has

a room in the house of M. Roselt, a merchant, where
I come and sit.   They say the Duque del Parque's
army (formerly Ballesteros's) is on its march to join
Elio's in Murcia and Valencia, and that Murray's is
to go to Cataluña ; ours has a great deal of sickness,
especially agues, and the hospitals here are full.
Several officers of the Sicilian troops (Austrians they
say) have resigned, and are returning disgusted with
the inactivity of this army ; in short, from its harle-
quin composition, parties, and misunderstandings, I
fear little can ever be expected from it.   Parque, too,
is an old woman, and no soul, Spanish or English,
places a grain of confidence in him.   Report says,
Ballesteros through the medium of Lord Wellington
is returning to take the command of that army, a
complete penitent ; he is excessively popular with the
soldiers and peasantry, but though he has undoubted
courage, loves his country, and never spares himself,
yet from being entirely without education, he is unfit
for an independent command ; with a brigade, and
even a division, and under the orders of a good general,
I believe he would acquit himself well, but ambition in his uneducated mind destroys his judg-
ment, and, of course, all his little merits.   Elio is

P

well spoken of, and I believe a fair general, but he is unprovisioned, and unassisted by his Government, and when he endeavours to draw provisions forcibly from the country he occupies, to which he is compelled by necessity and the neglect of his Government, these same idle fellows severely reprimand him for breaking the constitution. The Spanish battalions lost previous to the battle of Castalla, were obliged to surrender in their garrisons of Villena and Yecla, from not having literally a day's provisions. Henry O'Donnell, who commands the Army of Reserve in Seville, is a fine fellow and a good soldier. That army is well clothed, and they are a fine body of men, I think 12,000. Castaños is a good sort of old fellow, and amazingly popular among the Spaniards, but his merits as an officer are imaginary, and his fame entirely acquired by a series of extraordinary good fortune. He deserves just as much merit from the battle of Baylen as I do ; and it is the same in all other instances ; he himself, personally commanding, never did anything. Mina, in the north, is a fine fellow, the only clever man who has shown himself by the Revolution ; he was, they say, a blacksmith, and certainly was very low in life, then a guerilla, and now a Mariscal de Campo (Major

General), and second in command of Mendizabel's army. If he ever rises to the independent command of an army, probably he may lose himself, like Ballesteros. Lacy, who is gone to command the army of Galicia, is well spoken of. He was in the French service, and being ill-treated, came over to the Spaniards, his countrymen. All these Spanish *armies*, as they are called, amount together to a small number : they are generally ill-clothed, worse appointed, and still worse officered. The only effective corps are, I believe, Whittingham's and Roche's—perhaps 10,000 ; O'Donnell's reserve of 12,000 ; and one or two regiments raised and drilled by Doyle—these last are extremely good. This is what I have been enabled to collect during my tour through Spain, and as far as I can judge, it is the truth, but I may be deceived. The Catalans are a noble people—the perseverance of their guerilla parties has been truly surprising. I enclose a plan of the bridge of Alcantara ; it is a bad one, and will give you very little idea of the grandeur of its appearance, being simply an elevation intended for scientific persons ; however, you may like to see it. I have translated the explanations. I don't know yet when we shall go from hence.

&c., &c.

 WROTE you a letter from hence, my dearest mother, begun soon after our arrival, and continued for several days. I filled several sheets of paper to you, and sent a good many letters through my father to other people ; but as I know these letters were on board the " Malta" when she sailed a week ago with the expedition to Tarragona, probably this letter will reach you first. We had given up all hopes of Madrid, and had made up our minds to take the first opportunity that might occur to Mahon. None, however, offering for a long time, Madrid again haunted us as the time of Lord Wellington's advance drew nearer. Vague reports came here a few days ago that the capital was

evacuated on the night of the 27th ult., and entered the following day by Empecinado and his Spaniards, which was all confirmed yesterday ; and we shall start on Saturday for our long wished-for goal. We intend to go with very little baggage. We shall hire two calesas, and buy two horses. We shall take our two servants, which, with the Spaniards who drive the calesas, make six persons. In Madrid we shall once more join John, who I hope we shall keep steady in future. We shall leave his servant here with our luggage, and get the consul, Mr. Attey, to send him with it to Mahon in a merchant vessel or transport. We shall stay at Madrid about a fortnight, then go to see the Escurial, Toledo, and Aranjuez, and return to the east coast to embark. We hope that Valencia will then be open. We have no news from the expedition yet ; they sailed on the 31st ult. Immediately on our troops quitting Castalla, and coming here to embark, Suchet began his march northward with great part of his troops to meet us wherever we may go, leaving 10,000 to watch the Spaniards under Parque—4,000 of which are since gone; but Parque with his 25,000 has not dared to attack them : however, they say he has been waiting for provisions, and is now about to advance; if the French resist him, I dare say they will thrash him; moreover they have behind them a very strong pass, between Albaida (their advanced post) and San Felipe; thence they can only be driven by being turned at Fuente de Higuera; however, with Parque's immense superiority of numbers, he must indeed be an *old woman* if he cannot turn them. Never were poor mortals so dead sick of a place, as Clive and I are of this insufferable, stupid, filthy town; and our spirits are quite enlivened at the thoughts of our trip to Madrid. John Cobb has had a slight attack of fever. I find he had a similar one last year in London, which I never knew of, and a very trifling one at Badajoz; this last attack was more considerable, and he was unwell for three or four days, but is now quite set up again; just as he was recovering I had a little attack of cholera morbus, but I have had no return of it since the first day, and I am also well again; however, I look to leaving this oven, and to change of air and exercise, as necessary to re-establish us completely. Clive, even, does not prosper here entirely, although he has had no real complaint. Our letters from Madrid will be written in a very different tone;

we shall be eight days on our journey, and hope to reach that place on the 17th or 18th. I have received three letters from you.

&c., &c.

ERE, at last, we are all three arrived. Clive and I reached it on the 19th, and found John had anticipated us by some days—nearly a fortnight. There is but one other Englishman, whose name is Bonar—no great shakes, but of course we live a good deal together. He was the first Englishman that entered the place, being here five or six days before John. Our journey from Alicante was without incident, and we performed it according to the agreement I mentioned in my last letter from thence, in eight days. We soon perceived we had left that suffocating climate, were delighted more than I can describe to find ourselves again amongst the dear Castilians, and to hear once more their pure and beautiful language. We had a fine re-

freshing air the last six days, and arrived here with
our strength and spirits perfectly recruited. I was
rather disappointed in the beauty of this town, having
heard it so extravagantly extolled ; but all I have
ever heard of the patriotism, good feeling, and enchanting manners of its inhabitants, fell far short of what
I found them to be—I firmly believe them to be the
first set of people on the face of the earth. The popularity of the English exceeds anything I could have
conceived. We cannot stir without the blessings of
the people ; everywhere our ears are saluted with
" Viva Inglaterra ! " " Vivan los Ingleses ! " &c., &c.
Even the ladies, whose superior situation in life prevents
their expressing themselves thus, make their children
repeat these sentences. Oh ! how proud does all this
make me feel of my country !—the champion of the
world against the insatiable ambition and brutal tyranny
of Napoleon and his host of slaves ! A very few days
after our arrival the news came of the battle of Vittoria.
For three days the town was illuminated, the *Te Deum*
was sung in all the churches, the regiment of Don
Juan Martin, the Empecinado, quartered here, fired
feux de joie, and the happiness of the people was excessive ; the whole population passed the greater part

Q

of the three nights in the streets, the lower orders dancing, and singing patriotic songs; the women almost devoured us in the streets. The poverty and misery here exceeds, I think, all I have before seen; but the poorest beggars seemed to forget their misery and their hunger, in the recovery of their freedom, and the successes of their country—indeed, their joy seemed almost to exceed that of the other classes. I am all admiration, on seeing this defenceless town, which has not a wall so good as the poorest garden wall in England, to recollect that these rashly patriotic people could defend themselves for a single instant against Bonaparte, and his immense army; it seems to me that a Holkham shooting party with their fourteen double-barrelled guns, would be able to level this wall to the ground. Two bull-fights have been allowed in consequence of our late victory—the first took place last Sunday, and I suppose the other will be next Sunday. On account of the want of cavalry horses, they were not permitted to use any, as horses sometimes lose their lives in these fights; of course, therefore, we had it not in perfection; more-over, notwithstanding the mad passion of the Spaniards for this amusement, such is the poverty

of Madrid, that few persons were able to pay for a
seat, the amphitheatre was therefore not half filled ;
however, the scene was very gay and pretty.   One
bull only out of the ten was allowed to be killed, on
account of the scarcity of meat : this was most unskil-
fully performed, so that the poor animal suffered a
good deal ; but if well done by a skilful Matador (as
the man is called) the death is instantaneous ; and as
the person seldom fails, I do not think these much
talked of bull-fights are *so* cruel as they seem to be to
those who have not seen them, although they cannot
fail of being cruel ; but there is something very fine
and noble in the sport, which induces one to look
over the cruelty of it.

Tho' I have said I was disappointed in the beauty
of Madrid, I mean only to compare that beauty to
the expectations I was taught to raise ; it is certainly
a beautiful town, but very unequally so ; the public
walks, called the Prado, are most delightful avenues,
and adorned with numerous magnificent fountains—
this on the festival days used to be crowded with
carriages, like Hyde Park ; now if a shabby solitary
coach jogs slowly by, it causes a remark. The greater
part of the nobility and gentry fled from Madrid in

1808, all the remainder that were not entirely devoted to the French left it before the latter entered it last November, and the French party fled with Joseph, the other day; society, therefore, is not to be found here.   A few gentlemen's families of little note remain, but they are scarcely to be found in the great void.   You can form no idea of the robberies and destruction the French have committed, chiefly on their going away this last time—the desolate state of the great houses, the ruins which meet your eye on all sides, of the Retiro, the convents, magnificent barracks, &c., &c., added to the numbers of starving wretches who crowd the streets and walks, make at one moment one's heart ache; while (singular contrast) the air rings with joyful shouts and expressions of almost universal delight at the bright prospect which now opens upon them.   The new palace is a beautiful building, as far as it goes, but it has never been nor ever will be finished.   Another beautiful building on the Prado, intended for the Museum of Natural History and Arts, is likewise quite unfinished, and has been terribly injured by the French; indeed, the new palace seems to be the only thing they have at all respected.   From thence they have contented themselves with carrying off the *very* superior pictures, leaving still a very large and a very fine collection.   The houses of the grandees have disappointed me.   The only two handsome ones are —that formerly the Duchess of Alva's, and afterwards belonged to the brother of Godoy, Prince of Peace, and that of the Duke of Berwick, Alva, and Liria. These two excepted, the rest, though many of them *very* large, are neither handsome externally nor internally; the rooms are not fine, and the communications, staircases, and whole style, abominable.   The convents of monks are destroyed ; some are pulled down, but of most of them the walls are standing. One only appears to have been handsome.   Most of the nuns' convents are uninjured ; two or three have been pulled down, but near thirty still remain and retain their prisoners.   Some of these are good buildings, but that is all that can be said.   Of the public buildings the handsomest are the Custom House and Post Office, which are both *very* fine.   The General Hospital is not half built, and looks like a ruin.   Had the plan for it been completed it would have been a little town in size, and handsome.   The new museum, two immense barracks, and other buildings ruined by the French, are easily reparable; but probably will remain years in this ruined state. There is no such thing as a handsome square in Madrid. Two of the gates are beautiful, and two others very neat. Most of the roads for some distance are planted with avenues, but otherwise the environs are open and bare of trees. The mountains to the north and north-west are a fine object.

July 10*th.*—Poor Bonar received Tuesday last the account of the horrid murder of his father and mother, and immediately set off by Lisbon for England; we know not the particulars of it. We got the dispatches of the battle of Vittoria yesterday in the " Cadiz Gazette," but no names of killed and wounded; but Fitzroy Somerset writes John word that William is well, and an officer (Captain Hay), who is lately arrived here from the army, says the Guards were not engaged. No letter has come either from Orlando or William. We went the other day to the Escurial, twenty-eight miles from hence; it is a frightful building, but of immense size; it had the finest collection of original pictures in Spain, but the French have not left a thing of any description in the building. It is absurd to call it a palace, for there is nothing of the kind, only a few miserable rooms for the King and Queen when they come there. All the rest is a Geronine Convent, two hundred friars, all driven out by the French, which one cannot regret, as the riches of these fellows were abominable. We have already exceeded the time we proposed staying at Madrid, having been here three weeks to-day ; but the heat makes us idle, and some of the sights are not to be seen without trouble ; however, we shall certainly be gone before another week expires. We now know for certain that the French are out of Valencia, where we shall be in the course of three weeks. I could write you whole volumes on Spanish affairs, but you cannot feel about them as we do ; you have English politics to employ you, we hear nothing of them. Lord Fitzroy, in his letter to John, mentions the Catholic question being thrown out ; things go on rather ill, I fear, in Germany. Suchet and Clausel have joined at, or near, Zaragoza, making a force of 30,000, but Lord Wellington despises them. Pamplona is strong, its garrison is 3,000, besides 2,000 wounded left behind. I suppose Joseph will collect guns in France, and return to the field. He and Jourdan are two fools ; the other French generals are quite mad at being under their command.

The Cortes have voted Lord Wellington an estate, and the Regency are to choose it for him. The Spaniards have fought well in this battle, which is pleasant. Sir John Murray has played the devil; was there ever anything equal to his conduct? I hope Lord William Bentinck will retrieve our fame. I have got some Spanish music here, which I will send the first opportunity. I hope you will receive my two letters from Alicante. We are to have a better bull-fight to-morrow, with horses, and all that is right. I shall send this letter to Corunna—I fear it will cost immensely, but S——t would see me and you at the D——l before *he* would forward it, (I have heard enough of his character,) and Cadiz is such a round. I was walking in the streets this morning, and among a string of prints on a wall for sale, I recognized the picture over the hall chimney-piece at Weston, sup-posed to be the portrait of a Lord Arundel and his son; it proves to be a copy of a Vandyck, and the subject is Don Alfonso de Guzman the Good, first Lord of San Lucar de Barrameda, and founder of the House of Medina Sidonia; as the print was engraved in 1789, by Manuel Salvador Carmona, the original is probably now in Spain in possession of the Duke of

Medina Sidonia. I will send this print with the music from Mahon or Malta.

July 13*th.*—I yesterday saw the original picture; it is in the palace of the Marques de Villa Franca, heir to the titles and estates of Medina Sidonia. It is very beautiful, but has been damaged, and is in a very inferior state of preservation to yours. I could collect from the steward that the family set great value upon it. King Joseph had marked it to be carried away, and they know not by what good luck it has been left. We leave this place for Toledo on Saturday next. Mr. Frederick North and four friends are arrived here, they confirm the report we had heard that the plague is at Malta; I trust, however, it will prove trifling. They came from Sicily to Alicante. Sir J. Murray is almost hooted, and Lord William Bentinck was received with enthusiasm. We had a regular bull-fight on Sunday, and my opinion of it is totally changed; such a horrid scene of bloodshed and brutality in a country calling itself civilized I could not have imagined possible; but I won't attempt to describe it, for it would make you shudder.

God bless you, &c., &c.

R

OH! my beloved mother, what a large share of the happiness of my life do I see myself deprived of by the premature death of my dear and ever-to-be-lamented cousin.[1] Had it pleased God to let her remain in this uncertain world until she had reached the natural age allotted to us mortals, how many of the most peaceful and happiest hours of my life should I have passed in her society and that of her amiable husband! but the Almighty willed otherwise. She had suffered much from weak health, which she had borne with angelic patience and cheerfulness, and He has taken her away

---

[1] Harriet, wife of the Honourable C. A. Pelham, afterwards Earl of Yarborough.

to reward her virtues with everlasting bliss. The death of my dear grandfather was a blow to me at first, but that was an event to be expected in the natural course of things ; he had lived to a good old age, and when he was almost unable to enjoy anything in this life, he was taken to a better. When I last took leave of him it was with a strong presentiment that I should not see him more. How different is the case of my beloved cousin Harriet ! The last hours I remained in my native land were passed in her society ; she was in better health, and stronger, than she had been since she married. I received from her then, as ever, innumerable marks of her affection ; she accompanied me in the boat to put me on board the fleet as it passed Cowes, and afterwards came to Yarmouth, where our fleet had put back, to take leave of me once more. Here we parted for the last time ! Gracious God ! how little did I then imagine that I should see her no more. Nothing now seems possible to supply the loss to me, and I see myself, before I have completed my twenty-fourth year, deprived for ever of one of the chief sources of my earthly happiness. And yet my loss is inferior to my poor Lucy's, and, oh ! how they both sink almost to nothing when I consider that of her doating and disconsolate husband! May the all-merciful Father of mankind support him through this trial, which, I fear, will nearly overpower him. Clive received a few lines the day before yesterday from my aunt Bath, through Cadiz, in which at the end she just mentions that she fears I shall be much affected to hear of poor Harriet's death—this is all I have heard of it, for my letters are gone, I fancy, either to Malta or Sicily; but yet I was not quite unprepared for this melancholy blow, for at twelve o'clock on the night of the 16th of July, which was only five hours previous to our leaving Madrid, Bayning[1] and Herbert arrived there, and the former brought me a packet from Commissioner Fraser containing your letters Nos. 24 and 25 of the 15th and 19th of May, in which you gave me such melancholy accounts of my beloved cousin, that I ought to have resigned from that moment all hopes of her surviving—but while there's life there's hope, and I could not at once bring my mind to expect that so great a calamity was so soon to befall me— and I vainly hoped that in so young a constitution,

---

[1] Charles, second Lord Bayning.

the effects of this illness might not be fatal. Alas! alas! how vain was the illusion! I had intended not to have written to you till I had got to Mahon, but this melancholy news has determined me to get Clive to send this through Cadiz, as I think you will get it rather sooner, and the principal object of it is, that as poor dear Pelham,[1] since the death of William Cavendish,[2] has considered me as his greatest friend, and knowing his character as I do, I think it possible that he might in his present affliction receive some comfort from my society; in which case I would most willingly go home, and the greatest satisfaction I could experience would be in feeling that I was in the slightest degree able to lighten the weight of sorrow with which God has been pleased to afflict him. I cannot bear to think how long it will be ere I can receive your answer to this, and at times I feel almost determined to go home at once without waiting for your opinion, and yet I don't like to do an absurd thing; perhaps I might be after all of no use, and for

---

[1] The Honourable Charles Anderson Pelham, created Earl of Yarborough.

[2] Mr. William Cavendish, father of the present Duke of Devonshire.

myself I am infinitely better abroad—for here I am surrounded by no melancholy objects to bring my misfortune to my recollection ; on the contrary, every-thing I see or hear tends to make me forget England, home, and all belonging to them, and it is only at moments when my different senses are unemployed, that my reflections overwhelm me ; generally I feel myself bewildered by a sort of stupid melancholy, the cause of which I seem hardly to be aware of, which prevents me from enjoying surrounding objects ; while they on the other hand draw me away from the recollection of my loss. But why do I thus wound you with my melancholy thoughts ? If poor Pelham should ever express a wish for me, or from any hint, or anything else, you should imagine that I could be any comfort to him, write to me immediately, and I will return by the first opportunity ; indeed I trust you will do so should it occur, even without receiving this letter ; and after all, if on further reflection I should think it better not to wait for your answer, I may go home from Mahon.

I will now shortly answer your last letters, my be-loved mother, and mention our proceedings : we left Madrid on the 17th of July, for Toledo, whence we came straight here ; this journey, owing to the badness of the roads, took us a fortnight, and we arrived here on the 30th. Since then we have been detained here, owing to a report of the plague having been brought to Mahon from Malta—it turns out to be only one vessel in the lazaretto which has had a few sick, and it has proceeded no farther. We are now waiting for an English fish merchant-brig which is unloading here, and will then proceed in ballast to Palma in Majorca ; this vessel will take us all very well, and she expects to go in about a week. Herbert has now joined us, I have already mentioned his arrival at Madrid with Bayning, they stayed there a fortnight, and then Bayning went to England, and Herbert came here. I believe you don't know Bayning, I wish you would get acquainted with him, for I am sure you would like him ; he is very lively, sensible, natural, and agreeable, and one of the most honourable, conscientious young men I know. I have the greatest regard for him, and I believe he has for me. He went to Santander hoping to catch Mr. F. North and his party there, and to embark with him for England— would to God that I had by inspiration determined to have gone with him ; but I did not even read your

letters mentioning dear Harriet's illness till on my
road to Toledo, for I had not time the night I received
them, and as it was, I only was in bed two hours. A
thousand thanks, my dear mother, for them both. . .
. . . . I trust you will have received at last
my letter from Malaga. I have not heard from
Orlando since I left Alicante; I wrote him two letters
from Madrid, but I got no answer—he probably
thought I should not stay there so long; I shall be
most anxious till I hear something of him, though I
don't believe he could have been either in the battle
of Vittoria, or that of Pamplona. What a great man
is Lord Wellington, and how noble has been the conduct of all our troops; but it is dreadful to think of
the loss in two such bloody battles. Once more Lord
William Bentinck has raised the blockade of Tarragona, and they say the French had evacuated it and
blown up the works—this seems strange ; our falling
back appears to be owing to the Spanish troops wanting provisions; how abominable this is in those
whose business it is to supply them, with such a land
of milk and honey behind them as this province of
Valencia. John Russell goes with us to Sicily, and
intends to embark there for England in December.

I wrote you a long letter from Madrid by the post. I do not yet know whether the books I sent from Gibraltar, or the sherry I sent to my father from Cadiz, have arrived.   I must now close my letter hastily, dear mother,

&c., &c.

VALENCIA,
September 8th, 1813.

INCE I wrote last to you, my dearest mother, I have heard by a captain of the Navy, who came from Gibraltar, that Fraser has been so unwell as to apply for leave to go home. If this is true, in all probability you will know it long before you receive this ; but on the *possibility* of the reverse, I write these few lines to beg of you not to send any more letters through him, but to Sicily at once. I hope all those that have been sent to Malta will not be destroyed in consequence of the plague ; for old as most of them are, I long to read them all. I remain in the same mind as when I wrote last, about not going home until I receive your answer in Sicily. Oh ! my dear mother, how I long to hear some account of poor Harriet's

last moments (I pray to God that they may have been easy, and that her poor surviving, doating husband may have been supported through his hard trial). As is usual with everything relating to the sea, we have been delayed here a long while, but at last we are likely to go; our merchant brig sails to-morrow evening, we shall stay very few days in Majorca, and proceed to Mahon, whence I will write to you again. The unprovisioned state of the Spanish Army is quite melancholy, it did oblige us again to retire from Tarragona, and allowed the French to blow up the works; the poor soldiers are absolutely starving here in the midst of plenty; nobody but those on the spot, and who know the Spanish character, could believe their unnatural indolence and negligence possible. The Constitution, unfortunately, is so strict, that generals and commanding officers are absolutely forbidden to interfere in the provisioning of their corps, they dare not lay their hands upon a crumb of bread, and the civil authorities whose duty it is to supply the armies, think no more of it, than the inhabitants of the moon; yet the Government never thinks of punishing them, and the Cortes have been, and continue to be, solely occupied in disputing, and making laws for that country which they take not a single step to liberate, or secure, from their crafty enemies; it is enough to exhaust the patience of Job himself, to see their absurd and lethargic policy. Our troops are frequently put on half rations to save the poor Spanish soldiers from starving, yet all does not do to enable them to keep the field. How very flattering the Prince Regent's letter to Lord Wellington is; numerous inveterate cabals are already at work against him with all their venom, and I fear he will individually rue the day he took the command of the army of the haughtiest nation upon earth. The estate they have given him of the "Soto de Roma," is worth, they say, about $20,000 per annum; they first said 100,000, but that is an egregious exaggeration. Adieu, my dear parents; the wind, what there is of it, is favourable to us, but I imagine we shall have a slow passage.

. MAHON,
September 26th, 1813.

OB SPENCER[1] has just arrived from the fleet, my dearest mother, and has brought me your letters from the 6th to 11th July, and of the 17th, with inclosures from my dear father, Lucy, and poor Pelham. Lord William Bentinck, who is on his return to Sicily in consequence of some serious disturbance there, brought them to the fleet from Tarragona. Bob Spencer's brig has not entered the port, and he is going out to her immediately to proceed to England, so that I am quite bewildered how to answer the most important parts of your letters. I grieve much that you don't receive my long letter from Alicante, for besides con-

---

[1] Captain the Honourable Sir Robert Spencer, R.N.

taining so much of our travels, whole sheets were full
of interests which none but you and I and a very few
others should see. I was a fool to write so confiden-
tially from abroad. My letter from Malaga only
described some beautiful scenery and a few other
trifles; but as Fraser positively wrote me he had
forwarded it, I am surprised it has not reached you.
It has been a great comfort to me to receive your
detailed account of poor Harriet's last moments, and
that Pelham has borne all so well; but from his letter
I think it seems but too evident that a fixed despair will prey upon him, and that is a thousand
times more cruel than all those violent feelings he
seems to have escaped. However, I am relieved from
all doubt as to the necessity of going home to him,
although I still request that should he at any time
seem to desire to have me, you will instantly inform
me. Poor Mrs. Eliot's death I chanced to see in an
" Observer" at Valencia. Clive knew nothing of it.
I cannot say how much it shocked me. Oh! what
would I not give to have time to write comfortably.
I should fill a volume. Bob Spencer will take home
some Valencia shawls for me, and the Spanish music
so long promised. Poor Lucy's letter is very melan-

choly; she will never cease to feel her loss. My kindest love and duty to my father and her, and thanks for their letters. We are to have forty days quarantine at Palermo. It has almost made me forswear travelling, and I had half determined to go home. John is going; Spencer will disembark him in Tarragona, whence he will proceed by land to Corunna. A store-ship goes home in a few days, by which I will write fully. We arrived at Mahon on Thursday last, the 23rd; how, you shall know in my next. At present there is no opportunity to Sicily. I find by your letter that Orlando did not go with General Stopford to the army as he wrote me word he was to do, which accounts for my not having heard from him at Madrid. Pray send the enclosed scrap to Pelham, and tell him how I am circumstanced. In haste, adieu.

 WAS most cruelly hurried, my dearest mother, when I wrote you those few lines the day before yesterday by Bob Spencer, who commands the " Espoir" brig. I will now endeavour to reply quietly to your letters. . . . . . They say we shall have forty days quarantine at Palermo. I fancy we shall go in a transport which will sail in a few days; but as it is sure to have convoy, one of us may have the luck to go in the brig of war. Admiral Pickmore is very civil and obliging about our passage, and will do his best for us. We are living with the navy here, and go to many Spanish houses in the evening. The natives are stupid; many cannot talk Spanish, and the rest talk it very ill; but there are crowds of

refugees, chiefly Catalans, and some of them are pleasant. Spencer promised to get four Valencia shawls over for me if he could, and will send them to Grosvenor Street. Three of them, which resemble feathers, are peculiar to Valencia, and highly valued by some people ; the other I thought pretty. Everything I send home, you will know, my dear mother, you are welcome to ; and I must insist on your taking one of the crimson shawls, and the common one besides, and keep those you don't take for me till we meet. I bought a very long gold chain at Cadiz, which I intend for dear Lucy, but it has gone to Palermo, and I must explain why. A report was spread at Valencia, while we were there, that the plague had broken out *here*. On this John sent off a letter to his servant (who was here) to go to Palermo by the first opportunity with all our things, and he unfortunately went ten days before we arrived, so that we are in great distress for clothes (that is, linen) for the voyage. The report was false, and a malicious one, attributed to our enemies, for the place has been perfectly healthy ; and it is particularly unlucky for John, to whom we are to send his servant and things, on our arrival at Palermo.

T

Wednesday, the 29*th.* — I quitted you suddenly
yesterday, my dear Mother, for I found it was past
the dinner hour. I must conclude my letter to-day,
as they tell me the store-ship sails to-morrow. I
wrote yesterday to poor Pelham. Heaven grant my
letter may be some comfort to him ! I fear he suffers
more than he appears to do, and that his grief is of
that nature that rather stupefies than admits of out-
ward show of feeling, as we witnessed in him on poor
William Cavendish's death. Yours giving an account
of dear Harriet's, alludes to a severe illness Pelham
has had, the account of which, I suppose, is in one of
your letters that has not reached me ; thank God her
death was so easy and calm ! The want of feeling
she shewed on all occasions for some time previous to
it, is a melancholy subject for reflection—that a heart
so sensible as hers was, could be reduced by suffering
to almost insensibility ! Oh ! my dear Mother, how
young I am to feel so out of conceit with this world
as I already do. . . . . . .   This d—d place,
Sebastian, has cost us cruelly. I was very sorry indeed to hear of poor Cadogan's [1] death ; he is a great

---

[1] Hon. Henry Cadogan, killed at the battle of Vittoria.

loss; Fletcher's[1] is irreparable. I see by the papers
that Trant is gone to England. I wish it may be in
your power to show him some civility in return for
the very great kindness we received from him in
Oporto. I was greatly shocked to hear of Mrs. Eliot's
death. I read it in a paper at Valencia an hour or
two before we embarked, and I broke it to Clive at
Palma. We went on board our brig at Valencia on
the night of the 9th ; the wind was at first favourable,
but afterwards variable, with calms. The brig was a
clumsy, bad sailer, and the master a great blackguard.
We had a great deal of swell, and were all sick ; we
slept in pigeon-holes, like those in a packet, and
anchored at Palma at noon on the 12th. They gave
us a day's quarantine, and we went on shore the following evening. We had sent off our passport to the
Captain-General of the Province before, and they
treated us most magnificently. We lodged in the
Episcopal Palace, where they fed us very well. One
day we dined with the Captain-General (the Marquis
de Coupigny). Palma is a handsome old town ; we

---

[1] Lieutenant-Colonel Sir Richard Fletcher, killed before San
Sebastian.

stayed four days there, and amused ourselves very well. We then went across the island to Soller, and thence by Pollenza to Alcudia. The environs of Palma, and all the south of the island, is flat, but rich in olives and other fruit trees. Soller is the most beautiful orange garden, surrounded by the most magnificent mountains imaginable, and the views from thence to Pollenza are strikingly grand. Such magnificent mountains in so small an island are very remarkable, but it would be in vain to attempt the description of these natural beauties; I must defer this till we meet. We embarked at Alcudia in the morning of the 21st in a small fishing boat, not the size of a man-of-war's launch; but the wind being against us, we could do little, and towards evening we put into a small creek, near the mouth of the bay. Here we cooked our dinners, and laid down upon the shingles till past midnight. We embarked again at one, and put to sea with a favourable wind; but when we had got about half way to Minorca, these poor fishermen were desperately frightened, and lowered the sail, leaving us to be tossed about in a high swell wherever the waves chose to carry us; for a terrible storm of thunder had been threatening us all night from the north, and the wind freshened, and was variable and unsettled, the lightning incessant; and they said they must wait to see which way the wind would blow in the morning : in half an hour it was twilight; and shortly after the storm went off in another direction. After a little rain we got a fair wind, and the weather gradually clearing, we saw the low land of Minorca. Again the wind entirely failed us, and we lay becalmed for some time, but at last a light air slowly brought us into the Creek of Ciudadela at about eleven o'clock. In truth we had not a very agreeable passage, and were not sorry to change our clothes, and get some breakfast. With a good wind the passage from Alcudia to Ciudadela is made in three or four hours, and we were twenty-six ! I hope we shall have no more fishing-boat voyages. On the 23rd we arrived here. Minorca is a flat, ugly island, full of stones and empty of trees : Mahon is an excellent town, cheerful and clean, and there is some good quiet society, but no large parties. Clive has just told me the transport we expected to go in to Palermo has received orders to stay here, so that when we shall go is very uncertain. Lady Oxford is here, but as she lives a mile and a half off (at Villa

Carlos, otherwise Charles's Town), and I have no great predilection for her ladyship, I have not called upon her.   Clive dined with her yesterday.   Lord Oxford is gone to Cagliari, and she wants now to follow him, but cannot get a passage ; nobody seems inclined to assist her.   You expect accounts of the fêtes, &c., at Madrid ; but although we went there, certainly at an excellent moment to see the *lower* orders, it was quite empty of rank and fortune—consequently there were no diversions : but I particularly enjoy seeing and observing the *people* of a country, more especially in Spain, where they are the only estimable part of the population ; I don't mean *only* the *very* lowest.   God bless you, my dear parents ; give my love to all who care for me.

&c., &c., &c.

, MAHON,
October 11th, 1813.

E are still here, my dear mother, without any prospect of getting on at present. The "Redwing," Captain Sir John Sinclair, sailed yesterday for Cagliari, and took Lady Oxford and her family there, where they will join Lord Oxford ; they took no convoy, or we might have got a passage in one of them ; Sinclair proceeds from Cagliari straight to Malta, to take convoy to England. There are several merchant vessels and transports laden here for Palermo and Syracuse, but Admiral Pickmore has nothing to send to convoy them. We had a pic-nic the other day, some navy captains and we travellers, and enjoyed ourselves tolerably well: it would have succeeded to perfection, but the Consul's daughter (a young lady

of some consequence on such occasions) chose to be huffed about something; and when, at dusk, we expected to have had a dance she would go home, and she carried her point. . . . . . . We dine to-day with Admiral Pickmore, where we shall have a large naval party; he lives in a country house about two miles from Mahon. I begin to tire of this place, and so do the others. The society don't improve upon us; it will have a great loss to-day in a lady of the name of Taverne, who is going to Palma about a lawsuit: I like her and her family better than any Spaniards I have seen; she is a Catalan: her husband is a Frenchman who has always been in the Spanish service: he commands one of the Spanish line-of-battle ships which are laying rotting in this port. They have two daughters grown up, and several other children, and have music every night. The mother is a woman ·of education, and has brought up her daughters very differently from any Spaniards I have seen before, and they are capable of some other conversation than what you meet with in general in Spain, which is immodest love-making and disgusting flattery. The father stays here, as he cannot leave his ship, and the daughters stay likewise; but I fear we shall find the house very different without the mother. There are many amiable points in the female Spanish character—they are affable to strangers, and *very* good-humoured, and you can hardly expect conversation or good conduct from poor girls who literally cannot be said to know how to read and write ; the men are chiefly to blame here, and I hope the day will come when a general education throughout the country will render all more enlightened, and that the female part will be enabled to profit of those talents which they possess to a high degree ; they are infinitely superior in this country to our sex. I don't know whether the toasts *à l'anglaise* would astonish the Oporto ladies, but I am sure they have not that effect on those at Cadiz, where they are well used to them, and enjoy the custom beyond measure ; you would be shocked to see girls of fifteen, sixteen, and seventeen, swilling down bumpers of champagne one after another as they do. You mention how little summer you have had this year in England ; it has been the same here, and the rains and cold weather lasted so long, the people were quite astonished ; now it is oppressively hot, but at this season it is always variable, and they expect a great deal of rain ; as yet

U

there has been very little since we came. A few days
ago there was a dreadful storm, but it did not last
long—the thunder shook every ship and every house ;
one of the transports was struck with lightning which
carried away the main-top mast, splitting it into a
thousand pieces, injured the mainmast, killed two
men, and injured nine ; the storms here are tremendous, and accidents happen every year to our shipping in the harbour. The "Revenge" came in a
short time ago, and I have got acquainted with St.
John, one of its lieutenants, a great friend of Charles's ;
I dined with him the other day in the wardroom, and
it was very gratifying to hear Charles so highly spoken
of as he was by those officers who were with him in
the ship—there are few of them left, the greater part
quitted with Admiral Legge ; the "Revenge" is
now commanded by Sir J. Gore. St. John told me
he had seen the list of killed and wounded at the
taking of San Sebastian, and that Orlando was mentioned as slightly wounded ; I trust it is slightly, in
which case I shall rejoice at it, as there is nothing so
gratifying to a young officer interested in his profession as to have his name honourably mentioned. I
have seen the dispatch giving an account of this

affair, but not the list of killed and wounded ; it seems to have been one of the severest things our army have had. Poor dear Orlando ! God prosper him in his profession. St. John tells me he has no doubt Charles is acting commander before this time, as he knows he was second for promotion on the list, and we have heard some time ago of the first being promoted ; I wish St. John may prove correct. I am astonished I should not have mentioned Conway Seymour in my second letter from Alicante. He dined with us several times, he is a fine boy, very manly and sensible, and seems to like his profession exceedingly, he is rather forward, and plays the man, perhaps, a little too much, but then his conversation and remarks are beyond his years. I was very near writing once to Lady George, but I was too lazy, for I had written so much at Alicante that I was quite sick of it. Henry Thynne [1] spoke *well* of Conway, but I thought not with very great cordiality—but Henry is silent and quiet, and would not perhaps say all he thought ; they seem good friends.

October 17th.—I have now another letter to thank

---

[1] Lord Henry Thynne, afterwards Marquess of Bath.

you for, my dear mother; it is No. 29, of the 8th
of August; it came several days ago in a bag
directed to Alicante, which, most fortunately for me,
the Admiral's Lieutenant opened just before it was
sent to its destination, thinking it was possible there
might be a letter for some one here.   Fraser had sent
mine to the fleet, and directed it to Admiral Pickmore; but owing to some mistake, I had nearly lost
it—a thousand thanks for it, and its inclosures. . .
. . . . .   Don't fear any danger for me at Malta;
depend upon it, if they keep anything for me I may
safely receive it—for they are so cautious, they destroy
everything about which there is the slightest suspicion.
I am glad you have received my long letter from
Alicante, you say nothing of that from Malaga, which
must certainly be lost.

October 20th.—We are now likely to go to Palermo
in a day or two; the " Cossack," a twenty-gun ship,
is come in from Gibraltar, and is in quarantine, but
will convoy the transports I mentioned in my last
letter, without riding out here her quarantine. Captain
Napier is going to England, and will take this.   He
goes to Gibraltar in the " Stromboli " bomb-ship, and
sails to-morrow or the next day ; at Gibraltar he meets

the " Invincible," going to England. My next letter will
be from Sicily, where I fear we shall have a terrible
quarantine, although *this* place is perfectly healthy.
Captain Noel, who is going to join his brig in the
Adriatic, Herbert, Clive, and myself, are to have the
cabin of a transport to ourselves ; the master is to
feed us for a certain sum. I enclose letters for Lucy,
Mrs. Cautley, and Lord George Quin. We have such
strange, contradictory reports here of German affairs,
that it is impossible even to guess at the truth. I
trust, however, that all goes on pretty satisfactorily.
If I know the day of our sailing before I am obliged
to seal this, I will add it, if not, adieu. I had intended
writing to Mr. Chap, but I have not time ; give him
my love, and also to all my other friends and relations
you may see or write to. God bless you, my dear
parents,

> Your ever affectionate and dutiful son,
> G. A. F. H. B.

October 21*st.*—Nothing new has occurred, and I must
close up my letter. I suppose we shall go to-morrow
or the next day.

MAHON,
October 25th, 1813.

INCE closing my long letter a few days ago, my dearest father, our plans have been all adrift again. The convoy I said we were going in sailed yesterday, but Herbert was very unwell, and unable to go with it, and Clive and I do not like to leave him here; it is very unfortunate, for they have a delightful wind and beautiful weather. I directed my last letter (of which I consider this a P.S.) to Mr. Hamilton, at the Foreign Office, and this I shall direct immediately to you. I mention the circumstance in order that should you receive the P.S. before the letter, you may not think it is lost; they both go home by the same means, namely, by Captain Napier. Heaven knows when we shall go now; we are most heartily sick of

Mahon. The fleet are not come in yet, but are expected on the 1st, but the weather is now so fine again that possibly they may remain out longer. It will be a fine sight to see them all here together ; there are now seven line - of - battle ships, four frigates, and several brigs here, but that is thought nothing ! A squadron of five or six sail of the line are to cruise all the winter off Cape Creux and the Bay of Rosas. Sir J. Gore is to command as senior captain ; the ships are to be the " Revenge," " Ocean," " Berwick," " Fame," " Aboukir," and, I believe, another ; it will knock them about terribly. We are in anxious expectation of more news from the north, for we have heard nothing since Bonaparte entered Dresden. I am glad to find there was no foundation for the report of the yellow fever having shown itself at Cadiz ; at Gibraltar it is quite dreadful. The last accounts we have from Malta are much more favourable, and I hope the plague is now decreasing fast. God bless you, my dear parents,

&c., &c., &c.

HE "Perseus" is come in to-day from Algiers with M. A'Court, and sails again to-morrow for England. I will therefore send you a few lines, my dear parents, to say that at present all remains in *statu quo ;* neither Herbert being well enough to go yet, nor a means of conveyance offering, since the transports went that I mentioned in my last letter. I believe another opportunity for sending letters will offer in a day or two, when I will write again. The fleet are still out, but it is supposed they have left the blockade of Toulon, and are either on the coast of Catalonia or of Sardinia. We are most anxious for news that may be depended upon, both from the Peninsula and from Germany. It is an age since we have known

anything certain, and in the interval have been inundated with contradictory reports. My spirits are much better than they were. Clive would have written if I had not; this is some of *his* paper; he calls it letter paper, but I think it deserves the name of blotting paper better. God bless you, my dear parents, and preserve you, to watch over and guide

Your ever affectionate and dutiful son.

X

 WROTE you a few lines, my dear mother, last night, and sent them by the " Perseus." The " Repulse" sails to-morrow for the coast of Catalonia, from whence a ship is going home, and I take the opportunity of sending you a few more. I said last night that my spirits were much better, and I attribute it to two or three causes. *Time* is the principal one, I believe ; another is, that I heard from Captain Hamilton that his friend Clifford [1] is married to Miss Townshend, one of Lord John's daughters ; he could not tell me which it is, but I hope it is Audrey. I hear Harting-

---

[1] Admiral Sir Augustus Clifford, Bart., gentleman-usher of the black rod.

ton has made a very handsome settlement upon him.
This circumstance, however, cannot have had much to
do with the improvement of my spirits with respect
to the loss of dear Harriet. I attribute this more to
a rather singular friendship I have formed, which has
lately interested me a good deal, and in which I have
had the satisfaction of being of essential use to that
friend, against whom it seemed the world (at least
Mahon) was conspired; the gratitude of this person,
and the pleasure of feeling of use to a fellow-creature,
have afforded me comfort I have not experienced for
some time. This little circumstance seems to have
removed that gloom which had seized upon my spirits,
and although the immediate interest which had drove
it away, is itself passed by too, yet it has left a calm
behind, and I find my spirits wonderfully relieved;
don't think me quite out of my senses for writing such
an unintelligible story—the subject is such as I would
not trust to paper, though I would gladly tell it to
you; is it self-love that has led me to say what I
have? I hope not. I hope it is only the wish to give
you pleasure—you who are so kind as always to press
me to communicate all my interests. I grieve that at
such a distance I dare not be entirely unreserved. I

wonder what you will think of me—I begin to think myself a very odd fellow, and that I shall return to England a very different character from what I was two years ago. What I am most afraid of is, that I shall imbibe too bad an opinion of the world in general for my own happiness; I hope, at least, that I shall not become illiberal.

November 12th.—Contrary winds have detained the " Repulse," and yesterday the " Rivoli" arrived from England with papers to the 18th ult., bringing down the German news to the 19th of September ; upon the whole it is satisfactory, but we had raised our expectations higher. I see that poor Burrard, who I believe was the next above Orlando in the Guards, was killed at San Sebastian, at the same time that Orlando was slightly wounded. The " Barfleur" came in to-day from the fleet, and brings an account of the partial brush we have had with the French fleet of ten sail, as they were returning into Toulon. It is very unlucky that we could not bring off one ship. The *Moniteur* will make a flourishing story of it ; they say Sir Edward Pellew is very sore about it. The ship that is going home is the " Bombay ;" the " Repulse " will probably sail to-morrow, as the wind seems inclined to shift a little. The fleet is expected in daily. Herbert is getting better, and should an opportunity for Sicily offer in a week's time, I believe we may avail ourselves of it. I have written by this opportunity to my uncle Gunning.[1] Give my love to all you know are dear to me. God bless you, my beloved parents,

&c., &c., &c.

---

[1] Sir George Gunning, Bart.

In quarantine, on board the transport "Diadem,"
PALERMO BAY, *December 7th*, 1813.

MY DEAREST MOTHER,

N our arrival here, John's servant sent me
several letters from you. Thank you a
thousand times for them; they have
afforded me very great pleasure, but yet
I am not satisfied, for many are still missing. . . . .
Herbert being a great deal better, we embarked on
board the "Prévoyant" store-ship, which was to sail
from Mahon on the 24th ult. for Malta, touching at
Palermo; strong easterly winds, however, detained us
till the 27th, on which afternoon we sailed with a fair
wind, taking under convoy four transports and a merchant ship. We had an excellent passage with a
fresh easterly breeze, and anchored in this bay in the

afternoon of the 1st inst., exactly four days from
Mahon.   They put us into quarantine for twenty-six
melancholy days, making thirty from Mahon.   We
were rather thunderstruck at this information, but
upon the whole we bear it with becoming fortitude
and resignation.   The store-ship sailed on the 4th for
Malta, and we shifted on board this transport, one of
our convoy.   Our party in the " Prévoyant " consisted
of Lieutenant-Colonel Travers, of the 10th Foot,
coming on leave from Tarragona to see his wife here ;
Mr. Wilkinson, late secretary to Admiral Martin, going
to Malta, where he is appointed Agent Victualler ; a
Neapolitan gentleman, now resident in Sicily, who
spoke nothing but Italian ; Mr. Trounce, the master
of the ship ; and our three selves ; we were not therefore at all crowded, and formed a pleasant party
enough.   The first half-day we were all, except Wilkinson, very ill ; but afterwards, quite well.   J. Cobb
is in high feather, and desires me to say he does not
know how to thank you enough for all your kindness.
Clive is in perfect health, and thanks you for your
kind messages.   I shall destroy your little note to
John, as I imagine it cannot be worth returning.
Herbert is nearly recovered : I find from him that his

marriage with Ly. E. B. is certainly entirely broken off. You cannot think how glad we were to leave that abominable place, Mahon, after staying there nine weeks; I really thought it worse than Alicante, which is saying a great deal. After the fleet came in, we dined every day on board some ship,—with Sir Edward Pellew in the " Caledonia," Sir Sidney in the " Hibernia," Sir R. King in the " San Josef," with Captain Burlton in the " Boyne," and with Captain Hammond in the " Rivoli." I told Captain Burlton with what pleasure my father always talked of his passage with him to Ireland, and his great hospitality. He desired I would give his kind remembrance : he lives, they say, better than ever, and is the life and soul of the Fleet. Mr. and Mrs. Dashwood are still at Palermo ; he has kindly come out in a boat to talk to us almost every day, and has given us newspapers, &c., &c. John's servant has been extremely ill here, and is not yet much better; I fear he has had bad advice. I begged of Dashwood to send his servant to him to see that he got the best. I find he was kind enough to go himself, and George is now in the English military hospital, where I hope he will soon get well. We have got some books from shore, and are beginning to learn Italian, though I fear we shall not advance much by ourselves. Herbert learnt it at Malta, but he wants brushing-up. Colonel Travers is on board the "Iris" transport, where his wife and children have joined him, we three, and the Neapolitan, here. When Clive and I have grammared it a little, we shall find him of use to talk to, as Herbert already does. We are much delighted with the town and bay of Palermo, as we see them from our ship; nothing can be finer than the island appears; the weather is delightful, but this prison is not the place to enjoy it. Adieu till to-morrow, when I will resume my pen.

December 8th.—A transport arrived the other day from Ponza (the island near the Bay of Naples, taken lately by Captain Napier), bringing a despatch to Lord William Bentinck, and a Neapolitan gentleman, supposed to be sent with some proposals from his Government; the despatch was sent instantly to Lord William, and the transport returned yesterday to Ponza, with the Neapolitan, after a long conference between him and General McFarlane, now commanding here; the quarantine from Ponza here being forty days, he could not land. Yesterday brought us an account from

Y

Messina of another similar communication from the
opposite coast of Calabria, where a Neapolitan officer
had arrived from Naples; of course we shall know no
more particulars, but this is enough to raise favourable conjectures.   Our plans are to pass five weeks
at Palermo, and then to travel round the island, beginning at the west end of it, and thence by the south,
and east to Messina; but as we wish to be at the
capital during the greatest gaiety, which will naturally be in the carnival, we cannot determine finally
till we know when this falls; perhaps, therefore, we
may start soon from Palermo, make a short tour, and
return to it afterwards for a month; we probably shall
be near four months in the island, and then go to
Malta, from whence we shall go to Zante, and thence
to Greece.   In consequence of the time we have un-
expectedly spent in the Peninsula, I have persuaded
Clive to give up Egypt, though very reluctantly, for
he would fain see all the world, but I tell him I cannot remain so many years out of England.   He and
Herbert are still determined on going from Constanti-
nople to Russia—but I hope we shall have a Peace
by that time, when I should infinitely prefer visiting
Italy, Switzerland, and France.   All these are castles

in the air, but it is amusing to form plans for different circumstances.   They say the English are not near so popular here as they were ; Lord William Bentinck is much less so, since Sir J. M. was here, who seems to have conducted himself strangely, and to have shown great civilities to the French party, in short, to those who are Lord William B.'s chief enemies. The English are outrageous with him for this ; but he contrived to gain much popularity among the Sicilian nobility, and several of the authorities (those probably whom Lord William kept under rather more than they liked), but I know yet too little of Sicilian politics to speak with any confidence.   I will now answer some questions in a very old letter of yours, although too late, I fear, to be of interest: a Portuguese league *ought* to contain three miles and five-sixths, but I usually calculated them at four miles ; however, they are not measured, consequently you meet with no regularity ; they often exceed five, and sometimes are scarcely three ! A Spanish Legua del Rey (or King's league) is exactly four miles, but on the generality of roads they are not measured, and on an average do not exceed three and a half! A Quinta is the Portuguese name for a country house or villa, with a wood,

shrubbery, or garden enclosed by a wall; in Spain
they are less common, and are called Casas de Campo
(or country houses).   At the Convent of Arouca the
nuns who appeared at tea and breakfast were only
the Abbess and five or six old ones: it was in a large
parlour, divided by an iron grate, where they always
receive company of an evening; the eatables and
drinkables were passed to us by those turning shelves
common in all convents—I forget their name.   It was
at the grate of the church the next morning that we
saw the pretty young nun who smote Clive; her
sister, who is many years older than her, obtained
leave for her to come.   The Bernardine order is very
rich, and far from a strict one—these, and the Augus-
tines, fare sumptuously.   While I think of it, I will
say a few words about my letter of credit; it is dated
19th of June, 1812, to continue for two years; it will
expire, therefore, on the 19th of next June; the credit
is for £3,000, of which I have drawn, up to this day,
£500 only, and I am about £400 in debt to Clive;
after paying him, I shall have above £2,000 left—sufficient to last me a very long time.   I should imagine
that, without placing any new sum in Herries's hands,
I can have this letter renewed for two years longer.

As the packet calls at Palermo on its way to Malta, you may send any letters you write to me before the second week in March under cover to Lord William B., as we shall certainly remain in Sicily till late in April.   Direct afterwards straight to Malta. . . . . . . Gordon, of Xeres, is, as a politician, a great rogue, as Charles told you ; he was under arrest when we saw him there, but he has contrived to get enlarged since, I suppose by paying a sum of money to the Spanish Government—a common method there of wiping off the stain of treason.   Oh ! what corruption still poisons that unhappy country !   I am now come to that part of your letter in which you ask my opinion of the Roman Catholic churches and services.   There are certainly several things that inspire more awe than ours, but the heavy, gaudy, tasteless ornaments of them, together with the absurd monkey-like actions and motions of their priests, chanting or reciting like parrots, while their thoughts are employed in anything but devotion, never excite in me any feelings but those of derision or disgust.   They consider the organ a paltry instrument, fit only for common days (and even then it is but little played), and they seldom introduce its really religious tones amidst the numberless violins, violoncellos, &c., &c., on which they so furiously scrape.   Their grand days of music in Spain are called Funciones, one of which I saw at Seville, perhaps at the finest cathedral in the world—but any great fête in Spanish is called Funcion—a ball, fireworks, a night of illumination in a theatre, &c., &c.   You touch upon a tender string when you say how delighted I must have been with Seville.   I cannot forgive John and Clive for having deprived me of seeing Lisbon, and they bullied me again at Seville, for they would only stay there three rainy days, and ten, *at least*, are necessary to see all its fine buildings.   The Duquesa de Goa's daughter did not improve on acquaintance; she is an affected little puss, and her mother a great admirer of Soult and his countrymen—I wish they would make a few examples in Spain of such characters.   I have seen two vintages, but as they did not strike me as being either pretty or interesting, it never occurred to me to mention them.   I have never seen the Inquisition anywhere—idle enough of us ! The mule we left lame between Salamanca and Valladolid, recovered and joined us while we were at Salamanca the second time ; after various adventures, and just before both our muleteers decamped with a great many dollars—a strange mixture of honesty and roguery! John's servant remained at Oporto with most of our heavy baggage, and went by sea from thence to Cadiz. I remarked most of the things you cite from "Jacob's Travels :" the geraniums were in flower in the hedges of Chiclana when we passed them in January; but the beauty of that little town is almost destroyed by the French. I do not know the Oleander. Rice is not grown now in Malaga, but they continue the growth of the sugar-cane: I think I mentioned this in my letter from thence, but this letter you say has never reached you. I am glad my account of the Grandees' ball amused you. I don't believe Charles is quite right about the Duchess of Osuna ; she was formerly very fond of the French, and of French manners, but ever since the Revolution of 1808 she and her family have proved themselves very steady patriots ; she is a great *intrigante*, and far from an amiable woman, but clever, and a good Spaniard. God bless you my, dear parents.

&c., &c., &c.

Finished the 10th of December.

December 15*th.*—I have just learnt that the packet

for England is not yet gone, having waited for Lord
William Bentinck's letters. I should have written to
Lucy had I not thought it had sailed several days
ago. I enclose letters for Orlando, and Gally Knight.[1]
Lord William Bentinck is not yet returned, and I have
nothing to add. How glorious is the news from all
parts! There is a report here that Admiral Young
has taken the Scheldt Fleet—twelve sail of the line;
I hope it may prove true. The fall of Pampluna is a
great point gained. I hope we shall soon have a good
account of Suchet. If my box of books should ever
arrive in England, you had better open it, as it contains
my early journals, which may amuse you, and I am
not aware that they mention anything to shock female
delicacy; if they do, pray pardon me. You must
consider this sheet a P.S. to my last long letter. God
bless you once more, my dear parents.

---

[1] The late Henry Gally Knight, Esq., M.P.

PALERMO,
January 1st, 1814.

MUST begin, my dear father and mother, by wishing you a happy New Year; this is the second New Year's day that we have not passed together, and one more remains yet, but the fourth I trust we shall all be united again at Weston. You, my dear mother, I conceive to be now at Longleat, where I trust you are enjoying yourself; my father, I suppose, is in Ireland, and will, I guess, pass this day at Mount Shannon. I am passing mine quietly enough at this moment, but we are going to dine with Lord William at four o'clock, as there is to be a drawing room at six, at which we are to be presented. But I must go back a little and write regularly, or I shall forget many things. The packet sailed at last I think on the

z

22nd, by which I sent three envelopes, two of which
only I numbered; Lord William had not then returned,
but he arrived on the night of the 24th. I have got
three of your letters from him, Nos. 31, 32, and 33, for
which I trust I am as grateful as I ought to be for
your very great kindness in writing so fully and so
regularly. I begin to despair of the eight letters of
yours which I mentioned were missing in my last ;
the three directed to Stuart I have no idea of ever
getting, but I cannot help thinking the other five are
in some drawer of Lord William's, particularly as the
three I have got from him have been given to me at
different times. I am sure if Graham (his secretary)
would give himself the trouble of looking, he would
find more. No. 32 I received the first day after their
return ; No. 33 a day or two after, and I wondered
what had befallen No. 31, when last night at the
Opera he gave it to me. I asked if a packet had come
in, he said, " No." I asked, " How then did this letter
come ?" He replied, "I don't know." On opening it
I found it to be No. 31. This almost convinces me
he might find more by looking back for them ; it is
possible the packet from Malta may bring me some.
How tired you must be with this never-ceasing theme !

but you will conceive what an interesting one it is to me, and you will be interested yourself in the fate of your letters.

They excused us three days of our quarantine, and we trod on *terra firma* with considerable glee the 24th. I imagine Christmas-day was the cause of the indulgence we experienced. We were very fortunate to get on shore that day, for through the kindness of our friends Douglas and Dashwood (the former is Secretary of Legation, the latter, as you know, Pelham's brother-in-law), we were invited to a grand *fête* given by the Principe Butera, the First Baron (or Duke of Norfolk) of Sicily; he is rich, but immensely in debt, keeps open house, chiefly for the English, and seems very good-humoured and hospitable. His palace is very large, and the suite of rooms magnificent, and furnished in a very costly manner; we were about fifty at dinner, more than half English, and above one-third ladies. Many of the Sicilian nobles have adopted English hours, and the hour of dinner was nominally six; we sat down about seven! The dining room is immense, I think it must exceed 100 feet in length, and 50 in breadth and height; it was lit by 364 candles upon the tables and in the chandeliers;

there were two tables laid out, one for the dinner, and the other for the dessert—this has a grand effect, and I believe is almost peculiar to that house; we had even fresh napkins at the second table. We had not a service of plate, but yet the decorations of the tables were handsome. The dinner abounded in "quelque-choses," but there was nothing to satisfy an Englishman's stomach; the only substantial things were two turkeys, and I succeeded in getting part of the leg of one of them; the soup, and some of the dishes I tasted were not bad, but quite cold. There was hock, claret, and several Sicilian wines—some of which I thought pretty good; there were some excellent ices. We did not sit long after dinner; a great many people now came, who did not dine there, and after coffee we went into the concert-room, where we heard some good music; after which there were some English country dances, and waltzing. There was no regular supper, but cold meats, ices, &c. &c., in the refreshment room. We had not less than ten rooms open, and as brilliantly lighted in proportion to their sizes as the dining room. Prince Butera is a man of sixty at least, but the princess (who is a Neapolitan, and his second wife) is young, and by many thought

very pretty—I do not admire her. This place is very
scarce in female beauty, and I have not seen one
really pretty woman yet ; the party did not last very
late. I will not attempt to give any opinion of the
Sicilians at present, I will defer it for a future letter
when I shall have seen more of them. We have dined
with the Dashwoods, Orby Hunters, Douglas, Lord
William Bentinck, General McFarlane (second in
command here), and with a Chevalier Sauvaire, as he
calls himself—he is a Portuguese, and his estates are
in the Madeiras ; he is younger than me, was edu-
cated at Oxford, and was for a short time in the 10th
dragoons ; he has left the English service, and is
travelling, as he calls it — but, in fact, *residing* in
different towns ; he is good-natured, foolish, and ex-
travagant, fond of dress, and a servile imitator of
the English libertines of the day ; his friends find his
dinners and his opera box very convenient ; from his
name he must be of French extraction. H——t
having found a nature so congenial to his own, has
struck up an intimacy with him. H——t has another
friend here—the Prince of Lardaria (who, by the bye,
has a younger brother in England, who, it is said, is
to marry Miss Johnston, of Hanover Square). Prince

L. is a youngish man, good looking, well dressed, and a great imitator of the English; he has gentlemanly manners; but if one-fourth they say of him be true, he is the most unprincipled libertine that ever existed. He has been many years married—but they understand each other perfectly; indeed, this sort of agreement is pretty general here; he talks of going to England very soon, where I dare say he will take amazingly. H——t likes his horses and carriages, and they suit each other exactly.

We went to an inn on landing, where we remained a few days; we got very tolerable bed-rooms, but we were starved with cold—for there was no fire-place, and the wind came in on all sides; we only dined there once. The day before yesterday we removed to a very good lodging; it is the second floor of a house in the principal street, called the Via Toledo, or Cassaro, which, with another—the Via Macqueda—crossing it at right angles, divide the town into four distinct parts. We were obliged to engage this lodging for two months, for 125 dollars. Its furniture consists only of some tables and chairs, and three bedsteads for the servants; one of the rooms has a fire-place, which is a great comfort, for

the weather is very cold, though not quite equal to
England.   We dine to-morrow with Prince Butera ;
Monday with General Spencer; Tuesday with
Commissary Vaughan, whose wife is niece to Mrs.
Orby Hunter, and daughter to Mrs. Musters; Wednesday we dine with Major Kenah, D. A. General, by
which time I hope we shall have some more invitations.
John Cobb is quite well.   I enclose a letter from him
to his son Jack,[1] from whom you sent him one that has
pleased him very much—he showed it to me, it is very
well written, and most of the words rightly spelt.
The Dashwoods have been very civil and kind to me,
I like him very much, she has *quite* lost her shyness
since she married, which is astonishing.   I think she
was one of the shyest girls I ever knew.   She has a
slow, odd way of speaking, but seems clever and pleasant ; she is very fond of music, and I have heard
same very good at her house ; she is still very thin,
but seems in tolerable health though not stout ; they
have made the tour of the island, and she likes travelling.   They hope soon to be able to go to Italy, and
afterwards to Germany, Switzerland, and France, and

---

[1] Now (1875) a gardener at Weston.

propose to return to England in the autumn of 1816. There is plenty of Sicilian scandal, but the only English I hear, is of Mrs. O. H. and a younger son of Lord S——n. The Archbishop died suddenly yesterday, which caused a great sensation among the superstitious Sicilians; they say he was a bad one, and an inveterate enemy to England. Palermo is a dirty town, and most of the streets are crooked and narrow—this and the Via Macqueda are wider, straight, and handsome, and several houses looking over the Marina to the Bay are particularly so; and there are some very pretty ones to the south just outside the town; here most of the English live, and the view from their windows is beautiful. The Palace is an ugly old building; the cathedral a large pile of patch-work, it has some handsome marble pillars. Lord William Bentinck's house is not a good one, but it looks to the bay. General McFarlane's is a capital one, but it is in a street. The palace of the Prince of Belmonte is handsome, his and Prince Butera's are the only ones I have yet seen; their rooms are much finer and more comfortable than those in Spain. There is a pretty little opera house here, but the opera is very moderate; there are two other theatres which I hear are abominable. We went to Prince Butera's again last Friday evening ; he has music and dancing every Friday; his are the only Sicilian parties I hear of. There are public rooms over the Opera, where there are always conversazioni ; the Sicilians subscribe, but the English are admitted gratis. Mrs. Dashwood has little music parties every Monday. Books are so very dear here that I shall buy none but what I absolutely want ; I cannot hear of a good map of Sicily. We have got an Italian master, an Abate recommended by Dashwood—he seems a good little man ; there is no Tuscan or Roman here, so that you cannot meet with the pure pronunciation.

January 3rd.—I have this morning received your other letter of the 10th Oct., my dear mother ; it was negligent of Gibbs's people not to send it to me sooner —as it happened, you see, I got that which you sent through Fraser much the soonest. It could not cause any delay to send it through him, as the packets remain long enough at Gibraltar to admit of letters being opened and forwarded ; don't send any more through Lord William,[1] as I believe he will

---

[1] Lord William Bentinck.

soon quit Sicily on an expedition; send them after
the receipt of this to Mr. Hamilton, directing to me
to the care of the consul here, Mr. Fagan, and after
the middle of March to the care of the consul at
Malta.

We went to court on Saturday, and I never saw
anything so poor or so stupid; you do not kiss hands
on being presented, only bow. The Prince Regent
was in boots and regimentals; he is a little, fat, silly-
looking man. There were besides of the royal family,
the Princess Regent, who is also a little fatty, but has a
pleasing countenance, and when very young must have
been pretty—she is his second wife, and an Infanta
of Spain; the Duke and Duchess, and Mademoiselle
d'Orléans, and the Prince Regent's eldest daughter,
who is a child; the Duchesse d'Orléans is very plain,
and daughter to the King of Sicily; we had previously
been introduced to the duke, who had some days
before desired Douglas to bring us to him—he is a
very pleasing-mannered man; I never heard anything
more perfect than the English he speaks—how very
uncommon in a Frenchman! There were two or
three ladies-in-waiting, but no others came to the
drawing-room; the Princess and the other ladies were

dressed as at a common evening-party, some of them, indeed, had hats on.   There were a few men at court, those in uniform had boots, and were without powder; a few old courtiers were in full-dress coats.   The 12th of this month is the king's birthday, and I fancy the drawing-room will be better attended.   Prince Butera gave us a very good dinner yesterday, and quite a substantial one, we were about thirty persons; his way of living, and hospitality, are quite magnificent.

You were very lucky in hearing of Orlando through William Russell — what an excellent letter O.'s is, and how good you were to take the trouble of copying it for me.   I am surprised and sorry that Wolryche and Lucy have given up their idea of travelling; I am rejoiced, however, that the cause of it is her improved spirits—her last letter to me was by no means written in spirits—but I trust that was only a momentary melancholy.   William Childe gives me a long account of Madocks's affair.

January 5th.—We were driven yesterday four-in-hand by Prince Lardaria to see Bagheria, a village nine miles off, where many of the nobility have country houses; they cover the gentle rise of the promontory which divides the Bays of Palermo and Termini, and command very pretty views — most of the Lipari Islands are seen, too, from thence. The houses themselves are in bad taste, and destitute of trees, the gardens are laid out in parterres, and full of busts and statues ; one house belonging to the Prince of Palagonia, is justly styled, I think by Swinburne, the Palace of Folly ; the walls are covered in all directions with monsters, the most extraordinary that man could imagine, carved in stone ; Swinburne saw it in the late Prince's time—this man has pulled down three-fourths of them, but he has left enough to commemorate his father's folly. We are going to dine on Monday with the Duc d'Orléans.

There is an agreeable Frenchman here, of the name of Montrond, whom you may have known at Paris ; he was banished by Bonaparte, and went to Falmouth ; our Government would not permit him to remain in England, and after a short stay at Falmouth he came here, where he arrived eight months ago, bringing letters of recommendation from several Englishmen who knew him at Paris, among the rest, I think, Lord Grey and Lord Holland ; there is also a pleasant Frenchwoman here — a Madame Monjoie, who is attendant upon Mdlle. d'Orléans—she is unmarried,

but a Chanoinesse, they both live much with the
English. Madame Monjoie sings very well, and is
exceedingly good-humoured, and clever. Montrond
is a well-informed man, but a true Frenchman, and
terribly fond of ridicule; it is amusing to hear him
abuse Bonaparte, whom he abhors and despises as
much as he doats upon France. He says, " Est-il possible qu'il y ait encore un seul homme en Angle-
terre, qui pense que Bonaparte est un grand homme ?
c'est le plus grand fou qu'il y a dans le monde," &c. &c.
We dine to-day with the Dashwoods, and to-morrow
with Sir John Dalrymple, inspector of the Italian
Levey, who has a pretty little wife, an Isle of Wight
woman. Lord William's secretary, Graham,[1] went off
suddenly a few days ago in the " Furieuse " frigate;
he got a commission in the Italian Levey—became
Lord William's aide-de-camp, and disappeared all
in a minute; it is imagined he is gone on a military
mission to Naples. Secret expeditions are on foot;
General Montresor goes with the first division; but
it is expected Lord William himself will go with the
second. Every mouth is full of conjectures as to the

---

[1] The late Right Honourable Sir James Graham, Bart., M.P.

destination; I hope it may come to some good. Every day I hear Sir J. M.'s conduct more and more abused—how could ministers send such a man either here or to Spain?

Adieu, my dear parents,

&c., &c.

Y some ill luck, my dearest mother, the packet that arrived here on the 10th January, thirty days from Falmouth, brought me no letters from you or any one else, thus the latest date I have received from you is the 31st of October—an age ago. Another packet came in three days back, but as Lord Wm. Bentinck sailed the preceding evening for Naples (to whom I conceive my letters are under cover), I must wait either his return or that of some vessel ere I can have the satisfaction of hearing from you. I must, however, now tell you that the two first letters you wrote me in August and September, 1812 (Nos. 1 and 2) have at last found me—how, Heaven only knows!

Captain Mowbray, of the " Repulse," who arrived the
other day from Mahon, received them from Lieutenant
St. John, of the " Revenge " (Charles's friend, who, by
the way, I am happy to hear, is appointed to Admiral
Legge's ship), and this is all I know of these long-lost
letters. Would to Heaven that all the others may
some time or other reach me thus! I assure you
they gave me great satisfaction, notwithstanding
their old dates. Some persons to whom they alluded
of course called up my feelings a good deal, and made
me shed tears. Some amiable traits of dear Harriet
brought back her loss to my heart with all its bitter-
ness. Dear angelic cousin! where shall I ever find
so amiable a friend again! but I will not proceed.
. . . . But indeed
I am much happier now, and have lately gone on
in society quite comfortably. I have found great
pleasure in the quiet society of the Dashwoods, whom
I like better every day; she is an amiable little
creature. I am so angry with myself for having
weakly suffered you to think me so unhappy. I
would fain now persuade you to be comfortable about
me ; indeed, indeed, I am quite another person from
what I was a week or two back. I really now enjoy

myself very tolerably, and I trust that the tour of this island will amuse me and quite restore my happiness. Herbert is plaguing poor Clive a great deal, which keeps us here at present, and may yet detain us some weeks.   It grieves us to remain here wasting so much time, but this evil is not without its good, for the weather has been miserable, and is likely to continue so all this month and part of March, and the roads are nearly, if not quite, impassable from the heavy rains, so that our journey at present would be quite a penance ; yet I confess I grudge the time I lose at this stupid place instead of spending it at home, where I know your affection wishes for my return.   I am getting on in the meantime with my Italian, but am sorry to find that my fears about Spanish were too well grounded.   Already I bungle and find great difficulty in speaking the latter, while at the same time it confounds my Italian.   What would I not give to speak French, Italian, and Spanish well ! but I despair of it, my head is not clear enough ; however, I hope I shall always be able to read them, and that will be something.   I hope you have got my Spanish music from John, and the shawls from Bob Spencer.   I was astonished to see John's arrival in England about three weeks after he left us at Mahon—he *flew* home, on what wings I know not, but I suppose on those of political ambition. I saw by the same paper that William was appointed an A.D.C. to Lord Wellington. I have received a letter from Pelham written so long ago as the 8th of December; it is in answer to mine from Mahon, and, finally, puts me quite at ease about not getting home to him. . . . . Don't let what I have said of Herbert go beyond yourselves. Clive has still some hopes of getting him away, but I confess *I* have none. His tie at present here is the Princess Butera. What a hard thing it is to be linked to a person for whom I have scarcely a grain of feeling left! yet I feel sincerely for Lord and Lady Pembroke, who are miserable about him, and will do my utmost to save him. . . . . You can't think how hurt poor Clive is. Pelham has received the books Clive sent him, which went (or ought to have done so) from Gibraltar by the same conveyance as John's and mine,—his were for Lord Holland. It is a most cruel case losing them. I have a letter from Fraser of the 22nd January, in which he tells me he has made every inquiry of his people, who say that what things did not go with our servant to Alicante in the " Mermaid,"

Captain Dunn (viz., our travelling baggage), went home to England in the " Tortoise " store ship, as I wrote you word from Mahon. He says there is nothing of ours left in the dockyard store-room. The only way I can account for it is as follows:—the moment we left Gibraltar we all went with Fraser to look over our things in the store-room there; we wrote directions for our three boxes of books (as likewise John for a box of segars) on cards, and nailed them lightly on. Fraser promised us that these directions should be painted on the boxes; now, if he forgot this, John's cards and mine may have been knocked off and Clive's not, and thus, while Pelham's arrived safe, ours may be still on board or in the Custom House without a direction, and therefore unclaimed. Mine is a deal box about three feet long and two wide, with thongs of hide nailed round it. If there is such a one unclaimed and it could be opened, some of the books, if not all, have my name in them, and it could be thus discovered. John's box of books is much like mine, I believe. My journals are a cruel loss. In one of the papers by the last packet I hear my father is said to have gone over to Lord Clancarty in Holland. I am delighted to hear it. He

will be much interested, and if he is gone (as I suppose
he is) only for a short time, I can't help hoping he
has taken Henry with him. Dear Hal! what a
pleasure it would be to him.

I am very sorry to hear of all these militia regiments volunteering; I hope the Shropshire[1] has been
wiser. Heavens! are not our exertions in the common
cause great enough already, without endangering our
Constitution thus? Have we not a larger proportion
of men fighting compared with our population than
any other nation; besides paying the expenses of
Europe? Surely the successes of the allies have over-
turned steady John Bull's head; you cannot think
how frightened I am at home politics; you would
laugh to see me such a strenuous oppositionist. Now
is the time for your Whitbreads to be of real use to
their country in setting up popular cries, and they
seem to be struck dumb and quite stupefied by the
wonderful successes on the Continent;—even there
again, I have a hundred doubts and fears—I am sus-
picious of Austria. I am sure she is not well inclined

---

[1] Lord Bradford commanded the Shropshire militia.

to the general good; depend upon it she will prove ambitious and unjust. Oh! for the death of that arch-fiend Bonaparte! then, indeed, my fears would in a great measure subside. I have written some of my *new* politics to my Aunt Bath,[1] whose surprise I expect you will hear.

February 5*th*.—Nothing yet from Naples; but I must get my letters ready. I have really nothing to tell you about ourselves; we continue dining with the persons I named in my last letter, and our evenings pass at the opera or at Prince Butera's; lately, however, we have had some dances at General Gosselin's, Mrs. Vaughan's, and Douglas's,—generally it is the English country dance, with sometimes a reel, a little waltzing, and a bad quadrille. I don't find the Sicilians improve on acquaintance in any way; a little Spanish woman, wife of the Chargé-d'affaires, beats them all hollow—the pretty, graceful little figure is quite a pleasure to look at here, but her husband is so jealous of her that he never lets her show herself; I have only seen her twice, at the Princess Butera's and at Douglas's. The Princess

---

[1] Isabella, Marchioness of Bath.

Paterno, a very famed Sicilian, has been a very fine woman, but she is passed. Our weather lately has been wretchedly cold and damp. News from Naples is anxiously expected. I believe half the English here will remove there the moment it is open to them. The expedition remains in *statu quo ;* they expect to garrison some Neapolitan towns as a security for the treaty. Mrs. Cadogan and Lady Louisa were here for a long while; they went to Trieste a short time before our arrival, and are now, I believe, at Vienna. I understand they write that it is a most stupid place. I really believe we travellers think all places stupid while we are at them. You have no idea of Lady Louisa's popularity here ; the whole army to a man are in love with her. I found that I committed treason by saying her figure was not good ; she is thought the most beautiful, as well as the most charming of beings ; she accompanied Mrs. Dashwood in her tour of the island, and she seems to have formed a very just opinion of her—she is certainly a clever creature, and lays herself out to please.

February 10th.—Contrary winds have prevented the packet from coming round from Malta, and in the mean time Lord William has returned from Naples— he came on the 8th, and I had yesterday the satisfaction, my dearest mother, of receiving your letters, Nos. 34, 35, and 36, from the 13th November to the 27th December. I am cruelly disappointed to find that Charles has again returned to England unpromoted. Your anxiety about Orlando must have continued some days after you closed your letter to me ; the gazette, I think, was in the paper of the 30th ; those brought by the last packet reach fortunately to the 31st, so that I had the satisfaction of looking over the list of killed and wounded. This by-the-bye reminds me of the battles of the preceding month ; in the list of which I was sorry to see that both Mortimer and Meyrick were wounded—the former, poor fellow ! I think, was severely so—I shall be anxious to hear more of him from you ; I wonder you did not mention him in your letter from Longleat. Do not for an instant suppose, my beloved mother, that when I say I wonder at this, or at your not having acknowledged my letter from Madrid, I am capable of meaning a reproach—good heavens ! how far otherwise ! I am surprised, and most grateful to you for writing so much and so fully as you do. A thousand, thousand thanks for these last three letters, and for the almanack, which is a great treasure, and I looked forward to its arrival with pleasure, for I knew you would send me one. You enclose letters from dear Lucy and Henry, give him my love and many thanks ; if I have time before the packet sails, I will write to him ; I have written to Lucy, therefore I send no message to her. No, my dear mother, I have not been able to take the sacrament ; I believe it was administered here on Christmas day, but I only landed the preceding day, and I was ignorant of our having a chapel here till it was too late ; I have, however, had the satisfaction of going to church every Sunday, and after so long a deprivation, you cannot think how great a one it is. Lord William has made a treaty with Murat, as you will know ; the English may now go to Naples, and the Dashwoods, Orby Hunters, Lord Frederick Montague, and Stourton, will all go when opportunities offer ; Clive and I may, perhaps, run over to look at it for three or four days, if any one offers to take us. Herbert is kept in leading-strings by Princess Butera. I thought you were mistaken about the wine, which was with Clive's—I did not expect it to go home even by the same ship ; I am glad my father's has arrived safe, and I hope it will prove as good as it promised to be. I believe Costello, from whom I got it, is an honest man. The arrival of my books, too, is a real jubilee to me ; you will be sadly bored with my journal ; I wish I could point out to you the interesting parts to read—three-fourths of it must be *very tiresome.* I have written to Fraser to tell him of their arrival, and I hope my letter will find him in England. I wish my father may have been able to find General Trant ; his kindness to us was very great. Alas ! I was right in fearing that the melancholy style of some of my letters would give you pain ; I have been weak, but I will try to be more firm. Your last letters contain a great deal about dear, dear Harriet ; but I will not allow myself to comment upon them— I am now quite convinced that nothing does me so much harm as allowing myself to write all my feelings on that melancholy subject, the violence of them having considerably abated, I have more command over myself, and will endeavour to use that command. You say my letters lately have given you but little description of the country, &c., I have seen ; but, in truth, though other subjects may in a great measure have occupied my thoughts, and conduced to my silence on such subjects, yet I assure you I have seen little worth noticing, compared to the time that has elapsed since we were at Madrid. At Valencia, certainly, there was much to interest, particularly in the high cultivation of that district, and this I think I described ; so I did the beautiful country we rode through to the north of Majorca ; at Mahon, God knows there is nothing that deserves one line of remarks, neither do I see much here to amuse or interest ; however, perhaps I do not find interest in what some months ago would have occupied my mind considerably ; but since I left Castille I have not met with any interesting *people*, and this is what always delights me. How you would enjoy the Madrillanians ! I am glad the shawls are arrived safe, and I hope you will like them. I must have expressed myself ill about the music ; that which I sent from Mahon I got copied at Madrid, feeling how uncertain it was whether the gay Isnardi would think any more about his promise of sending you some from Cadiz. How fortunate Robert Gunning is to go out with Lord Clancarty as his secretary. John was very wrong to tell my father I was the worse for my travels—but I suppose you won't believe *me*. Clive

is writing you a letter, and I hope he will meet with
more credit. We are both as anxious as ever to see
Greece, notwithstanding the events on the continent,
and feeling that never was any one more deceived
than you have been by my mischievous cousin. I
hope I may consider myself at liberty to pursue my
travels there, as your request is only made on the
supposition that I am suffering from them; but I
promise you, that should I feel the worse for travelling
in Greece, I will go no farther than Athens. I wish I
may be able to persuade Clive to substitute Germany
for that stupid country Russia. Clive has got some
Sicilian agates for my Aunt Bath, and both he and I
have bought collections of agates and marbles for
ourselves—many of the former are beautiful; they
will go home with John's servant. I shall likewise
send by him the Spanish chain I have bought for
Lucy, also another box of Spanish books bought at
Valencia, and a few Italian from hence, as well as the
print of Guzman the Good, with some maps and plans.
I have bought here two necklaces made of a sort of
shell, and cut in imitation of cameos; they are poor
things, not worth their cost, but I am fond of anything peculiar to a country; they make them also at

Rome, and they say much better. Lord William Bentinck expects Lady William next month ; I hear she has been unwell, which is partly the cause of her returning to this warmer climate.

I have written such a long letter that I shall say little more on politics. I look forward to peace, if made now with Bonaparte, as the death-warrant of Europe; I am ashamed of our having treated with Murat ; he cannot but be a Frenchman in heart, and we shall suffer for it. The revolution in Holland does not go on as I could wish. I am convinced there is a strong French party, and if we make peace with that fiend Bonaparte, one of the first events of the next war would be the recovery of that country. Oh that the spirit of poor Moreau could rise and prevent the mad policy of Austria from taking effect! Clive, Dashwood, and myself, went on such a wild shooting scheme the other day that I am ashamed to give you an account of it,—we were rightly served for our folly by having no sport. We started immediately from Mrs. Vaughan's ball, went near twenty miles, part of the way in a carriage and the rest on horseback ; we began to shoot at daylight, and left off at one o'clock, about nine miles from this place, from whence we walked home to dinner; the last three miles it rained torrents, and we were drenched, besides being completely knocked up. We went in the carriage to a villa of Prince Butera's at Bagheria, where we breakfasted, and the night being very dark we proceeded by torch-light to the Chasse, about ten miles from the villa, on miserable horses, over mountains and roads unfit for human beings. At the Chasse we had about thirty men on foot (twelve of whom had guns, which was a hard thing upon us) and twenty dogs of all descriptions; we beat along the sides of a small river, and saw only a very few woodcocks and two snipes; Clive had but two shots and he killed his woodcock and snipe; Dashwood missed a woodcock, and I killed one, the only shot I got; the other twelve guns killed two woodcocks and some unhappy blackbirds and thrushes, larks, &c., which they considered fine fun, and were astonished we did not fire at them. Our sally forth from Villa Butera by torch-light in a night dark as chaos, accompanied by all these people (shouting like savages) and dogs, was the only amusing part of our day; the badness of the road, however, soon made us tire of this, and we were from half-past four till half-past eight reaching the river.

Adieu, my dearest mother, &c., &c.

We dined yesterday at the Prince Villafranca's; he is one of the Secretaries of State, and a very good-natured man. .They talk of his going as Minister to England next·spring. He and the princess, though young, are both uncommonly fat. She is one of the very few Sicilian wives whose character is good, and there are people who deny it to her. The Prince of Belmonte, who has always been considered as England's best friend here, appears to me to be the *proudest courtier* I ever saw. I mean these words to be understood in the fullest sense; his manners are so French, and there is something in them and in his countenance so deceitful, that I am persuaded he hates us in his heart most cordially. Few of the Sicilians see much of the English, and I believe we are very unpopular among the higher orders.

The perfect ignorance in which Lord William contrives to keep everybody here is quite extraordinary, and it is a great merit; but he has one failing, viz., partiality to foreigners, which he carries to an excess. There is a certain Catanelli on the staff of the Italian Levey who has immense weight with him. I believe he has talent, but he makes himself very obnoxious to the English in various ways, and gives himself in-

tolerable airs. He is supposed to be the planner of
all these expeditions, by the last of which we seem to
have made ourselves ridiculous enough. The navy
make a high joke of it. In short, I confess I think
the English have several just causes of complaint of
this sort, which I lament, because Lord William's
character stands so high in all other respects. Surely
after all Lord Wellington has performed with British
generals, engineers, &c., &c., it is hard to prefer
foreigners to them. What a bloody, but what a
glorious campaign this has been all over Europe! on
what a pinnacle of glory does Great Britain stand!
The English are said to be the proudest people on
earth, but they have a *right* to be so. Oh for an
historian worthy of recording to posterity the events
of the few last years! But are we not in the midst of
this good fortune forgetting our liberties and honour?
Our treaty with Sweden has sullied the latter, and
these strange Militia Bills are very like resigning the
former. I am not in England, where the general
feeling is on fire from the late glorious successes; I
am in a mean, enslaved little island of the Mediterranean, where I am more at liberty to reflect coolly
upon what passes in that Queen of the Atlantic, that

champion of universal liberty, to which, thanks inexpressible to the Great Creator, I have the happiness and glory to belong. They say that the Hereditary Prince of Sicily would not sign the treaty with Murat, which took Lord William over to Naples. I am sorry our Government will have anything to do with him.

PALERMO,
March 2nd, 1814.

 HAVE little to say to you, my dear mother, this post, and hardly a moment for that—the packet sails in a few hours; it arrived yesterday from Malta ; that from England, due a week ago, is not yet come in. Lord William and the first division of the expedition sailed on the 28th ult. We have had incessant rain for the last six weeks, but it is fine to-day, and rather promises to continue so. Clive and I begin our tour of Sicily to-morrow morning. I can say nothing of Herbert, but I neither expect nor hope he will go with us. I enclose a memorandum of the things I send home by John Russell's servant. I hope he will get my chain and necklaces safe to Heaton's. I foolishly

never thought of taking a memorandum of the contents of my box of books from Gibraltar, and I was equally thoughtless about that which I packed up at Valencia, and now I don't think it worth while to unpack it in order to take one. You shall have a full account of our tour from Messina; perhaps I may be able to write from Syracuse or Catania. My spirits are wonderfully better; I am more indebted to the Dashwoods than I can describe; there cannot be two more amiable beings, and their kindness to me has been excessive; she is really a most superior creature, and would suit you particularly. I have some hopes of meeting them again. The state of affairs in Italy is so uncertain, and so unpleasant, that it is most desirable they should not go there at present. The Orby Hunters have been at Naples some time, and we hear they are most uncomfortable, and very anxious to be back here. The Dashwoods have just thought of a plan which I hope they may execute: it is, to go almost immediately by sea to Messina, where Mrs. Dashwood would see Lady Sonnes,[1] whom she is very fond of, and she might either remain with her

---

[1] Sondes.

while Dashwood went to see Syracuse, which he missed in his tour, or, if the weather was fine, she might accompany him there by sea. From Messina they think of going to Zante, and by the Gulf of Lepanto to Athens; afterwards by the Adriatic to Vienna, before they go to Italy. The plan seems to me a delightful one, and very practicable, and it is of consequence that she should not remain at Palermo, which decidedly disagrees with her. Lord William has pledged himself to the ministers here to be back for the meeting of their new parliament early in April; it is quite absurd to see what babies they all are without him.

   God bless you, my beloved parents,
       &c., &c.

 WILL write you a short letter, my dear mother, from hence, although I am quite uncertain where I may be able to send it from, but having a little leisure time this evening, I can't employ it better than in writing to the best of mothers. We did not leave Palermo till the 4th, as our mules and horses did not appear on the morning of the 3rd until so late, that we feared not being able to accomplish the day's journey; our first and fourth days were rather bad and rainy, but the rest have been fine; owing, however, to the long and heavy rains that had previously fallen incessantly for many weeks, we found the roads (which are only horse paths at best), in such a deep and almost im-

passable state as an Englishman at home is really in-
capable of conceiving. Rivers, properly speaking, do
not exist in Sicily, but we found the rivulets (very few
of which have bridges) so swelled, deep, and rapid, as
to be nearly dangerous. Between Trapani and Marsala
we travelled miles together across flooded rivulets,
with a deep, tenacious mud at bottom, and the water
so thick and rapid that you could not see the bottom,
and suddenly changing from being shallow to a great
depth. That day two of the baggage mules fell in
the water, and my bed, John Cobb's, the cantine, and
some other things, were completely soaked ; we were
obliged to stay a day at Marsala to dry them, which
we fortunately succeeded completely in doing as it
proved a very fine one—and a fine day in these
countries is what you hardly know, unless you saw it
in the south of France when you were there. We
have generally gone to the locandas (or inns as they
are intended to be) in Sicily, and the one we were at
in Marsala was a good one of its kind, but yet the
bed they made up for me the first night was so bad
and so filthy that I could not sleep, and the next
night I slept in my own ; though that very morning
the mattress and every part of it was as wet as if it had

just been taken out of a river—and such is a Mediterranean sun, that I found it perfectly dry. From Marsala to this place we met with no particular accident, the River Platani, between Sciacca and Girgenti, was still so deep and rapid on the 11th, that we were forced to have men with strong poles to go through with us, and show us the ford, and that was the first day it had been passable for months—no small good fortune on our parts! We were to have proceeded again this morning on our journey, but it rained such torrents that we were obliged to defer proceeding till to-morrow; we were called at half-past five for that purpose, and you will hardly suppose it possible that it should be necessary to rise at that hour to perform a journey of eighteen miles. I will now return to Palermo, and tell you our days' journeys : on the 4th instant we went to Alcamo, thirty-one miles, but most of it good road; on the 5th we intended to reach Trapani, thirty miles, but were soon undeceived, and were obliged to stop at a farm-house half way, where we had the good fortune of being invited by a Sicilian, who happened to be travelling that road, and knew its possessor, otherwise we might have slept on the hills; our muleteers

wanted to cheat us finely ; on coming to the first ford,
we found it impassable, and they declared there was
no other, nor a bridge, on the whole river—however,
we found this to be a lie, from our above-mentioned
friend, who conducted us through some vineyards
knee-deep in mud, to a bridge about two miles lower
down. We went out of our road a little that day to
see the Temple of Segeste, all the columns of which,
thirty-six in number, with its entablature and pedi-
ments remain perfect ; it is of the Doric order, as are
all the temples in Sicily, and its columns not fluted—
its situation is fine, and commands an extensive view,
with the Bay of Castellamare to the north.   Only
think of these fifteen miles taking us eight hours !
On the 6th we reached Trapani (fifteen miles farther)
easily.   Monte San Giuliano, just above Trapani, was
the ancient Eryx—but not a vestige of the town or
of the famous Temple of Venus remains ; it is a fine,
bold, insulated mountain (though not equal to Monte
Pellegrino, near Palermo), and has a village at the
top with the remains of a very large Saracenic castle.
At Trapani is a famous coral fishery—I bought some
of the coral, but I don't think its colour is good.
Marsala was our next day, eighteen miles, which the

mules were eleven hours going; there is nothing picturesque or fine in this promontory—all this western part of Sicily is low and flat, and cultivated with corn and vines, with few trees; at Marsala there are some very extensive and extraordinary caves, parts of which are now used for making gunpowder; they extend miles, opening at short intervals to the air; they are all excavated by man, and indeed by some of the very early inhabitants of Sicily, they variously say by the Sicani, Siculi, and Phœnicians, possibly it might be the Saracens. On the 9th we went to Castel Vetrano, an ugly old town, but with a rich plain below it towards the south-east. This day's journey was twenty-four miles, and easily performed. On the 10th we went twenty-four miles further to Sciacca; Clive and I, however, went round to see the ruins of Selinuntum, eight miles from Castel Vetrano, close to the sea; there are the ruins of six temples, which have been thrown down by a violent earthquake—not one column now stands entire, but the greater part are discoverable on the ground, at least of the larger temples; many stones from the smaller ones have been carried away for building. The five smaller temples were all with fluted columns (the other, which was immense, and dedicated to Jupiter, had but very few fluted columns), some persons think therefore, from so odd a mixture, that it never was finished ; altogether these ruins are very interesting ; at present the spot (which then was so flourishing) is dreary and desolate—we saw no living creature, nor heard any sound but that of the sea.   Sciacca is a fine old town, and its situation and surrounding country beautiful ; the ground very varied and full of almond, caroba, and olive trees, and the sea view very extensive.   Near the town rises a rocky mountain called the San Calogero ; at its summit are some very extraordinary grottos, which are natural vapour baths ; they have been used medically ever since the time of Dædalus, who is said to have dis-covered them, and by whose name they are called ; a hot wind is continually rushing to the mouth of the grotto, which instantly covers any one approaching it with moisture all over ; we found the heat 92° ; the air is quite powerful, and the cause whence it may proceed invisible.   Near these grottos rises a hot sulphureous spring, which by a natural channel under ground supplies some ancient baths an immense distance below ; the heat of this water is 130¼° ; this

E E

is generally ascribed as the cause of the hot damp
wind from the grottos, but Denon (who gives a very
just and long account of this phenomenon) observes
that there is no smell whatever in this hot air, which
there would be if it was sulphureous—the fact is true
that there is no smell! At Sciacca we were lodged
in an Augustine convent, to the prior of which we had
a letter; we were very well treated by him. From
Sciacca we were two days coming here, without anything remarkable but the River Platani, that I have
before mentioned. On the 11th instant we went
twenty-four miles to the wretched village of Monte
Allegro, which deserves anything but its name, and
where we slept in filth and vermin; and eighteen
miles further brought us on the 12th to this place.
Here we find the inn a tolerable one. The situation
of Girgenti is magnificent, upon a high, steep, rocky
hill, overlooking a highly cultivated and beautiful
varied country, and an immense expanse of sea
beyond; the little rivers which wind along rocky
valleys, the great unevenness of the country, with the
numbers of almond and other trees, the richness of
the corn at this time of year, with the two beautiful
ruins of the temples of Juno and Concord, situated

on the most picturesque spots, and the mole, port,
and shipping, four miles off, make this vast picture
quite enchanting. Here the ruins are very different
from Selinuntum, being surrounded by farm-houses
and a busy multitude ; there are still to be seen ten
temples, but eight of these are in a worse state than
those at Selinuntum ; the Temple of Juno has its
thirteen northern columns standing entire, with the
entablature and several other columns variously
damaged ; the situation of this ruin is uncommonly
fine, and it is the most picturesque thing imaginable.
The Temple of Concord is not far from it, and is still
more entire than that of Segeste ; it has all its twenty-
four columns and inner walls, with two staircases—
in short, almost everything but the roof ; it gives one
a perfect idea of a Grecian temple. All the temples
of Agrigentum had fluted columns ; the temple of
Olympian Jupiter was perhaps the largest ever built ;
it is supposed to have had seventeen columns in length
and six in front—in all forty-two, and of gigantic
dimensions ; but then the circumferences of the pillars
were not of single stones, excepting the capitals, and
in this respect it must have been very inferior to the
smaller temples ; the small ones at Selinuntum had

not only the circumferences of the columns, but the whole entire columns, of single stones. There is a tolerable old cathedral here, in which is a famous sarcophagus, representing on its four sides the story of Phædra and Hippolitus; there is also a beautiful picture by Guido of the Virgin and Child, and some magnificent pieces of plate, extremely old.

CASTRO GIOVANNI,
March 19th, 1814.

 SHALL send this letter to Palermo from hence, my dear mother, as I am ignorant when the next packet will sail for England, and I should be sorry my letter was not in time for it. I shall send it under cover to Mr. Gibbs, Herries's correspondent, as the safest means I can think of. The post to Palermo goes to-morrow morning.

We left Girgenti on the 16th, and reached this place yesterday, sleeping at Canicatti and Caltanissetta; we had eighteen miles each of the three days; the first twenty-five miles the country was beautiful, since then it has been less so, but not ugly.

At Canicatti, which is an ugly town of 15,000 inhabitants, we were at the inn, which is not a bad one. At Caltanissetta we were in a Benedictine convent, to a brother of which we had a letter from the Duke of San Giovanni, in Palermo; it is a large, substantial old building, finely situated above the town (which itself covers a high hill) and commanding an extensive view. We were here remarkably well treated, and found our friend a well-informed, liberal, happy, fat man—his name is Giuseppe Scotti Cassinesi; all the Benedictines in Sicily are of noble families. Caltanissetta is a good town of 15,000 inhabitants also, but there is nothing remarkable in it, as we were told; the afternoon we were there was so rainy we could not stir from the convent. We arrived here on another equally miserable afternoon, and our poor animals were so tired with the deep and execrable roads, we were ourselves and our servants such drowned rats, and many of our things in such a wretched state, that we determined to remain here to-day. This is the ancient Enna, but no remains of antiquity exist, except the ruins of an immense old castle, and a singular octagonal tower—it is called the Tower of Piso, and the castle Saracenic.

I confess I believe them both to be Roman. The situation of this town is most singular—it is built upon the nearly level top of a rocky mountain, almost perpendicular on every side. It is so high that from the castle I could see plainly this morning the whole of Ætna, the sea near Catania to the east, and Licata to the S.S.W., the range of mountains running from Messina to Termini, and the following towns, viz., Calatascibetta, Traina, Leonforte, Asaro, San Filippi d'Argiro, Centorbi, Caropipi, Aidone, Mazzarino, Naro, Caltanissetta, and Sutera. If you will look at the map of Sicily, you will be astonished at the distance of some of these places. We have had no accident, or anything worth mentioning, since I wrote at Girgenti. We are all quite well and happy, and in hopes that after the new moon on the 21st we shall have fine weather. To-morrow we go to Piazza, the next day to Caltagirone, and then by Chiaramonte, Modica, Spaccaforno, and Noto, to Syracuse; there we shall stop about three days, and then proceed by Augusta to Catania. We hope to be able to see Mount Ætna, but we cannot know till we reach Catania; some people say it is easy in April, others, impossible; we shall afterwards go to Messina and embark for Malta. The Sicilians appear to me a sorry set of people—the nobles are illiterate, and little to be respected; in the middle orders I see no character at all; the lower orders are knavish, and more horridly filthy than anything you can imagine; the country is fertility itself, and seems to me much better cultivated than Spain; it is a beautiful island, good roads would make it quite a paradise. I never saw such ugly women as the Sicilians; the men are not ill-looking, but the women have bad figures, ugly faces, and dress abominably, without an atom of grace. The poultry throughout the island is exquisite; meat extremely scarce. I am so starved with cold I can hardly guide my pen; there are no windows to the room, and the air (which at this height is very keen) comes in at every direction; I will finish my letter after dinner.

Nine o'clock.—I am almost as cold as I was before dinner, and I must draw my letter to a close. We are just returned from the house of the director of the studies of this town. He is a learned and a most good-natured man, and has a small library of very valuable books, such as your Dukes of Devonshire and Marquesses of Blandford would give thousands

for.   He has also a collection of medals, chiefly
Sicilian, and a small one of mineralogy.

Adieu, my dear parents,

&c., &c.

(No. 30.)

 HAVE this morning, my dearest mother, received three more letters from you, all kindness as usual, which I hasten to offer you a thousand thanks for, and in dutiful obedience to your commands I will write you our proceedings since Castro Giovanni, before I answer them. I shall not have time to say much to-day, as we are going to hear some music, and are only waiting for a Mr. McDonald, a Scotch Roman Catholic, chaplain to the regiment "De Rolle" here, who is to take us to the house. Clive and I have been employed this morning in going to see the Scoglj dei Ciclopi, some curious insulated rocks a few miles from hence; they are entirely composed of lava, and one particularly

is an abrupt pyramid of basalt columns; the most
general opinion concerning them is that they proceeded from a small volcanic crater under the sea;
however, many people think that they are immediately
from Mount Etna; the former opinion seems to me
the only probable one, for why otherwise should they
be islands at some distance from the land, and with a
great depth of sea immediately at their feet? and
still more, how else should the basalt columns have
been formed, unless from the opposite forces of fire,
water, and air? There is nothing very striking in
their appearance, but I believe they are very great
natural curiosities.

We arrived here on the 1st, and have been very
much pleased with what we have seen at Catania; the
remains of the ancient city under ground (or more
properly speaking under a stratum of lava), of the
theatre, little theatre, amphitheatre, and public baths,
are very curious and interesting, and several very
valuable public and private museums and smaller
collections we have seen have very much gratified us.
The terra cotta vases in the museum of the Prince of
Biscari are quite beautiful—all but two were dug up
in Sicily; the museum contains besides an incal-

culable number of lamps and various house utensils of terra cotta, female ornaments of brass, household gods, great numbers of perfect and imperfect statues, some of which are of exquisite workmanship, fragments of the columns, friezes, &c., of the ancient theatre and other public buildings (the former of which must have been one of the most sumptuous and magnificent among the ancients), sarcophagi, an extensive collection of the productions of Etna and Vesuvius, and numerous other less interesting subjects; there is another general museum in the convent of Benedictine monks, but inferior to that of Biscari, though far from despicable. The Prince of Biscari has one of the finest collections of cameos in the world, but we have in vain endeavoured to get a sight of them; the present man has just succeeded to his titles and estates, and promises little to resemble his patriotic, liberal grandfather, who was one of the greatest benefactors to Sicily. But were I to give you such detailed accounts of all we have seen I should fill quires of paper, and tire you quite as much as myself. I will be more concise; it is all in my journal, where some time or other it may amuse you to dip a little.

This is a most magnificent town, quite composed of

fine palaces, churches, and convents; about one
hundred and twenty years ago it was levelled to the
ground by an earthquake, and most of the present
town has been built within these sixty years; many
of the churches are beautiful, and their altars composed of the most beautiful agates you can imagine—
all the productions of this country. A painted ceiling
of a church of Benedictine nuns is one of the handsomest things I ever saw. A priest who had some
money to spare amused himself with building a church
in exact imitation of Loretto, which encloses the supposed house of Joseph and Mary, miraculously
brought from Nazareth; here we have the church,
house, &c., inch by inch, as in Loretto, and it is
curious enough. All the environs of Catania being
of lava, is a most extraordinary sight—that of the
later eruptions remains black and bare, while the rest
is cultivated, but even here, the black rocks that remain not decomposed among the almonds, olives, &c.,
have a most singular appearance. I never could have
formed an idea of the effect of such a volcano, without
being an eye-witness to this strange country of the
Cyclops; the lava everywhere has the appearance of
mountains of cinders, still seeming hot, and so sharp

that it cuts your shoes all to pieces—it has still all the
shape which it had when a stream of fire, and gives
me an idea of whirlpools of burning matter suddenly
petrified and cooled, yet we know that it took an
astonishing number of years to cool.   We left Castro
Giovanni on the 20th of March, and arrived at
Modica, *via* Piazza, Caltagirone and Chiaramonte, on
the 23rd ; we did not see anything on our way worth
mentioning ; the roads continued horridly bad, and
the weather very rainy ; we were forced to ford deep
rapid rivers, and go out of our way for bridges, with
various other grievances, but without any accident.
The roads about Modica are solid rocks, with deep
holes worn in them, then filled with mud and water ;
our poor animals suffered much—they lost their shoes,
tore their hoofs, &c., and we were obliged to rest a
day at Modica ; we were there in a private house, to
which we had a letter, and were very civilly treated.
It is a good town in a most singular and picturesque
situation ; it occupies several narrow and almost perpendicular rocky valleys watered by rivulets ; on the
sides and in the bottoms of these valleys, industry has
made grow the prickly pear, with a few fruit trees,
and a little corn and garden stuff.   At the top of the

town is an old ruined castle, whence through the valley you discover the sea—all this pleases the traveller's eye, but is very inconvenient for the poor inhabitant. On the 25th we went to Noto; our servants and baggage went there straight, but Clive and I went out of our way to see some caves in a valley called Ispica—this valley is similar to that of Modica by nature, and a small brook runs along it, which passing by Spaccaforno soon after falls into the sea ; these caves are artificially but very rudely cut in the rocks on both sides of the valley, and there are one, two, three, and even more rows of them one above the other, according as the rock is more or less lofty ; they extend for a distance of at least nine miles, and must have contained a great number of in- habitants. One dwelling with three storeys of rooms, appears evidently to have been that of the prince or the chief of the people. The middle is the principal storey, and they ascended or descended to the other two through holes in the rock, there are no re- mains whatever of steps ; this dwelling is at this day inhabited by the principal shepherd of the country, and a few of the other caves by inferior ones ; they are usually called the Caves of the Siculi, but Denon,

in his " Travels through Sicily," conceives them to
have been made and first inhabited by the Sicani—a
still more ancient people, and afterwards successively
by divers other people, who in the numerous wars
of this ever-fertile island, found themselves worsted
and forced to seek shelter in hiding places ; his reason-
ing is exceedingly ingenious and plausible.   There
are some large sepulchral chambers, which are evidently of a more modern construction, probably
either Grecian or Carthaginian.   Perhaps these
caves are as interesting and as curious for an anti-
quarian as anything to be met with anywhere ; this
place seems to have remained down to the present
day as wild as when first inhabited, and the few
shepherds who now dwell in some of these
singular caves are possibly just as ignorant, though
less ferocious, than the Sicani or the Siculi.   It rained
torrents all the time we were examining these wild
dwellings, which greatly annoyed us, and diminished
the pleasure we should otherwise have enjoyed.   The
roads continued execrable ; my horse lost a shoe
miles from a blacksmith's shop, and I was forced to
creep along, sometimes mounted, sometimes on foot,
to the nearest village, which was seven miles off ; this,

through roads such as I described when speaking of
Modica, was no trifling distance. Having got the
shoe put on, I had proceeded a short way, when off
came another, and I was obliged to return to the
village; this also being put on, I exactly arrived at
the same spot, when it was off once more. I now
perceived that the rocky roads had so torn my horse's
hoof, that this was the cause of what at first appeared
witchcraft. A countryman who was accompanying
me from the village to put me into the right road was
so surprised and terrified, that he turned all colours,
exclaiming, "O! Giesu Maria!" and crossed himself
with great fervency. This amused me so much, that
my patience, which was ebbing fast, soon returned to
me, and we went once more to the village to repair
our loss. The blacksmith shod my horse with great
care, and as I soon after got into a good turf road, all
went on well. I must, however, add that I am con-
fident my guide took me for a necromancer, for though
I had engaged him to go as far with me as a bridge
six miles off, which he had undertaken with great
glee, we had hardly got a mile from the village, ere
he entreated me to let him return home, and seeing
that the road became better and less intricate, I parted

with the poor terrified man. Clive had continued his road quietly, and was quite astonished at the length of time I was in overtaking him. Although we left Modica at seven o'clock, and only went a distance of twenty-three miles, we did not reach Noto till some time after dark. Here we were lodged at the house of Prince Villadorata, to whom we had a letter from Dashwood, who knew him in Palermo. Clive's servant, who had gone on first, just caught him as he was going to his country house two miles off; however, he immediately ordered rooms for us, sent his cook and steward from the country, gave us an excellent supper, capital wines from his own vineyards, comfortable rooms and beds, and, in short, treated us like princes. I never saw so much comfort since I have been abroad, out of an English house; his principal man-servant is an Englishman. The Prince rode over the next morning while we were seeing the town, &c., of Noto; we had otherwise intended visiting him on our way to Syracuse, at his country house, to have thanked him. At Noto we saw one of the most extensive and valuable collections of coins perhaps anywhere to be met with—it belongs to an old Barone Astuto. Noto is a beautiful town, and quite modern, having been destroyed by the same earthquake that destroyed Catania ; it has several magnificent palaces and convents. I happened to go into a church belonging to a convent, where the nuns were singing to the organ—one of them had a beautiful voice, and sang several solo parts so divinely, that I could hardly quit the church some time after the voice had ceased, lest she should begin again, although I knew Clive would be waiting impatiently for me ; this was the first time that I was perfectly satisfied in a Roman Catholic church. I am sure I have not been so with any of the absurd ceremonies and tinsel magnificence I have seen here during this Passion Week. We only remained one night at Noto, the country about which is delightful, and by far the most desirable part of Sicily to live in, as far as I can judge from what I have seen ; the face of the country is very varied, the soil rich, plenty of springs and rivulets, corn, grass, almond, olive, and caroba trees, vineyards, and everything that is rich and cheerful.

We reached Syracuse on the 26th. This is a most interesting spot ; we spent two days in viewing the antiquities ; never was there a place that called to one's mind so distinctly the great events of history

that there took place; you can still trace the walls of
the ancient town (which extended between twenty
and thirty miles) nearly all round. The theatre and
part of the amphitheatre were cut out of the solid
rock, and therefore must last as long as the world.
The immense stone quarries, called Lautomia, in one
of which is that curious excavation called Dionysius's
Ear, the use and purport of which has so long been a
question among the doctors, and will in all probability
never be solved; the wonderful and magnificent sepulchral chambers, where thousands and thousands of
sepulchres are hollowed out of the solid rock on each
side of long passages deep under ground; the famous
port where the fate of Athens was decided; all
together, so many objects strike the eye at once, that
it is impossible to see Syracuse and not be for the
moment transported with enthusiastic feelings for
those wonderful Greeks. I know no place where so
many grand events of ancient history took place as
at Syracuse, consequently, no place in itself so interesting. There have been several beautiful fragments of statues found, others nearly entire, and one
or two quite so; within these few years one of Venus
was found, but unfortunately without the head and

the right arm; the position is nearly similar to that
of Medici, the proportions much larger; and it is a
question whether this is not superior in beauty; as
for myself I think it far the most beautiful statue I
ever beheld. Mr. McDonald has forgotten us, and I
have therefore been enabled to write to you a long
letter, but my neighbours in the adjoining rooms are
snoring so soundly that I must now bid you good
night, my dearest mother.

April 10*th*.—I will now resume where I left off.
The third day we were at Syracuse we took our guns
and a boat, and crossing the port went up the River
Anapus to the source of the famous fountain of Cyane;
this source is a large basin, clear as crystal, of above
twenty feet deep; the bottom appears of rock, per-
forated with innumerable holes and covered over with
moss; you see all the fish playing in it as if only the
purest crystal was between you and them; it is
singular that there is not the most minute bubble of
water distinguishable, nor anything that denotes a
spring, yet hence flows a very copious stream per-
petually, equal in summer as in winter, and taking its
course for four miles through marshy meadows, and
then through cultivated lands for half a mile more,

unites its clear, full stream with the muddy Anapus, a small river caused almost entirely by the melted snow and rains in the winter, and next to nothing in the summer; half a mile further the united streams empty themselves into the port of Syracuse. During the greater part of the course of the Cyane it preserves the same exquisite clearness as at its source, and from the great depth of its bed the stream is equally imperceptible; approaching the River Anapus, the bed becomes shallower, the banks steeper and closer to each other, the stream continues to be evident, and even strong, but gradually less limpid, though its superior clearness is strikingly remarkable till a little below its junction with the Anapus. In the middle of summer, and in the autumn, the Cyane is covered and quite concealed by weeds, notwithstanding its great depth. One of the most interesting things of this fountain is the plant of the papyrus, on which the ancients wrote instead of paper; this grows here in great abundance, and was recovered by the late Cavaliere Landolina Nava, of Syracuse, the royal custos of the antiquities of the Val di Noto and the Val Demoni, who prepared it in small quantities; his son, who has succeeded both to his office and merits, continues to do the same. We received great civilities from him and he gave to each of us a little bit of his prepared papyrus, inscribed with his name ; it is a beautiful feathering plant and grows in the water without attaching its roots either to the bottom or sides, receiving nourishment solely from the water. Nothing can be more simple than the manner of preparing it ; it is only cutting the stalk (which is pithy) into thin slices, which you form into the shape and size you wish to write upon ; then, laying these sheets under heavy weights for about a fortnight, it unites by its own succulency, and is ready for writing upon. Having passed three interesting days at Syracuse, on the 30th we came to Augusta, a miserable town, with a beautiful natural harbour, made no use of ; the surrounding country is rich and pretty. On the 31st we expected to reach Catania, only twenty-five miles, but on coming to the ferry of the River Giaretta or Simeto (anciently the Symæthus) we found it so much swelled with the rains and melted snow that they assured us we could not pass, for that the stream would force the cable and carry us all into the sea ; we therefore got into a small uninhabited house close by, bought some fowls and eels for supper, and con-

soled ourselves well enough, the night being fine ; the
next morning we passed over prosperously, and
arrived early at Catania.   Since this month began
the weather has been less rainy, but still unsettled
and disagreeable.   We are going to-morrow to
Lentini, eighteen miles off, to shoot for a couple of
days on some marshes and a lake of the Prince
Butera's ; the shooting in the winter is quite extraordinary—we shall be late, but still expect
good sport, for it never fails.   John Cobb has
had an attack similar to that he had at Alicante,
but less severe—he is   too unwell to go with us
to-morrow, and I leave him under the care of the
surgeon of De Rolle's regiment.   When we return
we   shall   make   an   attempt to see Etna, then
proceed by Taormina to Messina ; all here tell us
Etna is absolutely impracticable, but we shall go to
Nicolosi, a small place on the mountain where the
guides live, to ascertain the truth ; we are yet rather
sanguine, there is however a most formidable nightcap
of snow still upon it.   We are going to-night to a
dance with the Cavaliere Patemo, with whom we dine
at half-past three ; we shall then see the fair Catanese,
who are said to be pretty women.   Heaven knows, in

all the rest of Sicily they are ugly enough ! Among
the common people, they are absolute devils in filth
and ugliness, almost without exception ; nor among
the upper order of females at Palermo did I see anything strikingly pretty.   Catania has the greatest
fame ; it is singular that an island which so long and
so often formed part of the Spanish dominions should
bear so little resemblance to Spain ; it is true that in
the vulgar language you catch some corrupt Spanish
mixed with more corrupted Italian, but here the male
part of the common people are as mean as the
Spaniards are noble minded ; the females here are without beauty, figures, or grace, nor do you meet amongst
the upper orders with that affability, or the quickness
or liveliness, that you see in Spain ; the common
people here of both sexes are quite despicable, dirty,
mean, stupid, idle, ugly, unwilling, prejudiced—in
short, everything that can make man most contemptible
and revolting.   Among the gentry I have seen many
liberal, enlightened, patriotic, pleasing men, who have
their country's good at heart, and are truly grateful to
England for her steady assistance ; the nobility are
very, very bad.   I hear constantly from Dashwood,
and Mrs. D. was so kind as to write me word of poor

H H

little Harty Pelham's death, which I thus knew before I got your letters; hers was a most amiable one on the subject—I must consider it a fortunate event, and if you got all my letters from Mahon you will have seen that I wished it—but I am sorry poor Pelham feels it so much. Many thanks to dear Lucy for her letter. I cannot say how much I am annoyed to hear of poor Charles's ill-luck; all you say of Orlando is most satisfactory; you do not mention Henry—of course, you had nothing particular to tell me about him, but I like to see all their names in your letters. I should like to hear of Orlando's getting a staff appointment now that he has seen regimental service. I am sorry dear Mr. Chap has been so ill, and I don't like the account my uncle Gunning writes of himself. Thank you much for the books you are sending by A'Court. I shall write to Palermo that they may be forwarded to Malta. No, my dear mother, you will never see in me again that gay, thoughtless happiness I used to possess; it is now two years since I have lost that enviable feeling, and should the recollection of those events which deprived me of it gradually decrease and sink into oblivion, yet the

mind habituated to reflect upon its losses, could
only recover its former harmony by returning to the
age in which it lost it, and I shall never again be
two and twenty ; but, perhaps, it may yet please
the Almighty to give me a considerable share of
mortal happiness ; and that which He sees good to
deprive me of may render me more fit for eternity
and then be repaid tenfold.   But, alas, I cannot
flatter myself that since I have been less happy I
have been more virtuous—far, very far, from it.
This recalls to my mind that I had the misfortune
to lose, the other day, the ring you gave me, on
which was engraved in old orthography, "Let vertue
be thy guide ;" it was a very cold, rainy day, we
had to cross a river in a cockleshell-boat, while our
animals swam after us; for this, of course, it was
necessary to take off the saddles and bridles ; we
are always our own grooms, and I must have rubbed
off the ring in putting on the saddle again, my
hands being so numbed with the wet and cold, I
did not feel it at the time. I had not, however,
proceeded far before I missed it, but the banks of
the river being grassy, I conceived it would be in

vain to go back to look for it. And now adieu, my
dearest mother.

&c., &c.

[Two letters unfortunately are here missing—they
were from Messina, and one of them contained an
account of Mount Etna.—L. E. B.]

No. 33.

MY DEAREST MOTHER,

E arrived here yesterday morning in the "Trieste" merchant brig, three days from Messina, and I found some letters from you at General Maitland's, but as the packet sails to-day, I have not time to answer them. You will be surprised and sorry to hear I am going to England from hence. Since I arrived at Messina I have not been so well, and therefore Clive has persuaded me not to go on to Greece. Don't imagine now that I am very unwell; I assure you I am not, and probably after passing a short time in England, I shall go out again through France and join Clive either at Vienna or some other place. I hope to get a passage in a man-of-war, as several line-of-battle

ships are coming here to proceed to England ; should I fail in this, a packet is now at Palermo on its way here, and will be sailing for England in about a fortnight. I conceive you are abroad before this time, and I have written to Mr. Heaton and Mr. Hamilton to stop all letters they may receive for me ; of course if I should go abroad again before your return, I shall meet you somewhere, ere I join Clive. We had such a crowd of passengers on board our wretched brig, that nothing could be more uncomfortable than our passage from Messina. I have not time to write more by this packet, but I will write fully by the next, should I still be here. God bless you, my dearest mother.

&c., &c.

No. 34.

NOTHER packet came in on the 7th, my dearest mother, and brought me your letter No. 50, April 24th, with several enclosures. Out of the fifty letters you have written me, I have now received forty-four, which, taking all things into consideration, is fortunate. I find Spencer was at Gibraltar when the last packet touched there ; I conceive he had not got either your letter or the books, or he would surely have sent them to me by the packet.

E are at General Maitland's palace in the country, where he passes the summer, and where we came yesterday to pass a few days. There is a beautiful garden, and it is infinitely cooler and altogether pleasanter than Valletta. . . . . I will not enter much into politics, having little time, as the packet sails to-morrow; I will only say that England is in no way bound to the King of Sicily touching the restoration of Naples, nor do I imagine such a measure desirable, as the Bourbons were abhorred by the Neapolitans—but I do think that the Powers who restore to a Corsican robber the title of emperor, which he himself resigned, who give

the son of his wife (the discarded mistress of a revolu-
tionary tyrant) a petty sovereignty, and his butcher
of a brother-in-law such a kingdom as Naples, deserve to have their own crowns torn from their heads.
Was it before I wrote my last that we heard Herbert
was going from Sicily to join us at Zante? I think
not; Clive might have a pleasanter companion, but
he will be better than solitude, and I rejoice at it
now that I cannot accompany him. There were no
more carnival gaieties at Palermo than what I mentioned, except a few absurd masks in the streets, and
some very blackguard masquerades in the theatres.
In answer to your other question respecting our mad
shooting party from Palermo, the twelve other guns
were twelve clowns, being nothing more than a por-
tion of the thirty beaters; the villa is a tolerable
house in an ugly garden, in a still uglier country,
and the breakfast consisted of bread and butter, tea,
coffee, and tough cold fowls; we walked home eight
miles, because it was less fatiguing than riding rough
starved mules over bad roads and stony mountains
for nine or ten miles to the villa, whence we should
have had nine more to go in a carriage. We have
some very unpleasant accounts of the conduct of

I I

Ferdinand the Seventh, on his arrival at Valencia ;
if his proclamation as we have it be true, he is a fool
or a madman—if the Spaniards yield to him, they are
not what I took them for ; and if they resist, a most
bloody revolution must ensue ; the king will have the
whole army, the whole Church (perhaps the most
wealthy and numerous of any nation), and the greater
part of the grandees, with him ; against such antago-
nists, rivers of patriotic blood must flow ere they can
establish their independence.   Clive is still here, but
will go to Zante by the next packet.   The " Elizabeth " and the " Tremendous," line-of-battle ships, are
expected here from the Adriatic to go to England,
and General Maitland says he is certain Captain
Gower of the " Elizabeth " will give me a passage ;
but there is a report that she is to be the flag-ship at
Gibraltar, and that Captain Gower will give her up
there.   The " Weazle " sloop, Captain Noel, was
going home from hence, and Noel offered me a passage—but he has since been told he is to return to
the Adriatic.   I do not fancy so long a passage in a
packet, which is a very small brig, with bad accommodations.   The " Havannah " frigate is here waiting
for Hamilton, who has lately been appointed to her ; if

he comes before I have an opportunity, he will certainly
give me a lift to Gibraltar on his way to America, that
would be very pleasant, and it would be very unlucky
if I could not get a passage home among the numerous ships that will go from thence. General Maitland is uncommonly civil to us ; he has a rough sin-
cerity of manner which displeases many here, and he
does not promote gaiety enough for them ; but he is
very entertaining in his own house, and his household
are very good fellows ; his aides-de-camp are a son of
Lord Lauderdale, and a nephew of Sir David Baird ;
and his private secretary, a Mr. Plaskett.   This place
would suit you particularly; it is an irregular, large
house, between three and four miles from Valletta,
with a large, beautiful garden with terraces, and broad,
straight walks full of fruit and flowers. We have a
burning sun and a cloudless sky, with the finest evenings possible. The distance this place is from the
town makes it as retired as you please, and there are
rooms with every aspect. We breakfast at half-past
seven, dine at three, and walk all the evenings in the
garden. The Governor's palace in Valletta is magnificent ; he lives there in the winter, and has assemblies
every ten days. They tell us the Maltese society is

bad, but we have as yet seen nothing of it. Next Monday the General means to begin weekly parties, from half-past five till half-past eight in the evening, with dancing and refreshments in the garden ; it will be an extremely pretty scene, but we are not to expect any beauty, as they say the Maltese women are remarkably plain. I believe we shall go back to Valletta the day after to-morrow ; we have been here since last Monday, and I daresay we shall return here to stay again. The cultivation of Malta is wonderful, considering the rocky, barren spot it is by nature ; almost all the soil is brought from Sicily, yet almost every foot of the island is cultivated. The beauty of it this year is passed, as the clover and corn are got in ; but it still looks tolerably green from the quantity of figs, with some caroba trees, orange gardens, olives, and other fruit-trees. Valletta is the handsomest and best built town I ever saw, and the villages throughout the island are better built than most towns. The divisions of all the fields are stone walls which have an ugly appearance, and the whole island is low and flat. The population is about 120,000; 50,000 of which are in Valletta and its suburbs. The fortifications of these are immense; but from their extent they require a garrison of 50,000 men, a number that could never be provisioned. The harbours are beautiful, and there is a very pretty little dockyard; it is altogether a most extraordinary place, and well worth seeing. St. John's Church in Valletta is very handsome, and hung with beautiful tapestry; the floor is entirely composed of the different knights' tombstones, with their arms in mosaic, and they form the most singular and beautiful pavement I ever saw. We went yesterday to see St. Paul's Cave, in Città Vecchia, and some catacombs, which are very inferior to those at Syracuse. I believe we shall go this evening to St. Paul's Bay, where he was shipwrecked. A cousin of Wolryche is the commanding engineer here, and his sister Mary is with them; Mrs. W. is a clever woman, and they are altogether the pleasantest people here.

God bless you, dear mother.

LONDON,
August 26th, 1814.

MY DEAREST MOTHER,

 SAT down to write to you yesterday, and I accomplished a sheet of paper, but I was so dissatisfied with it that I have destroyed it; I hope I shall be able to do rather better to-day. I reached London the day before yesterday, from Deal, where I landed the preceding day. I will hasten to tell you that my health is perfectly recovered, and that you need not have an anxious thought about me. Would to God my mind were as much at ease as my body! But I will endeavour to confine myself as much as possible to matters of fact. I left Malta on the 21st of June with my friend Hamilton, who has got the "Havannah" (36 guns). We went to Mahon, where they put us

in forty days' quarantine. We remained but one day there and were ordered to Gibraltar, where we arrived on the 10th of July. There they put us in forty days' quarantine, but they were to reckon from the day we left Malta. This would have given us pratique on the 30th of July, but the " Havannah " was ordered to proceed to America, for which she sailed on the 19th. Fortunately the " Haughty " gun brig, Lieutenant Harvey, had lately arrived from Malta, from whence he had sailed the day after us. Mr. Harvey is well known to Hamilton, and came to dine with him. He kindly offered me a passage to England, and I removed from the " Havannah " to the " Haughty." We sailed from Gibraltar on the 22nd of July, with a small convoy ; we had contrary winds for three weeks, and anchored in the Downs on the 20th instant. We got pratique on the 23rd, and I arrived here the following day. No less than five of us slept in the little gun brig's cabin. I got a standing bed-place, so that I had the pleasure of the whole motion. However, I am an excellent sailor, and I had not a moment's sickness. I found several letters from you. . . . . I have seen nobody but Mr. Chap, who is very ill with the lumbago, and is so altered since I saw him that his looks shocked me. I hope you will not think of coming home on my account; perhaps I may go abroad again myself in a few months. Congratulate Charles for me on his promotion. I am glad Henry will see a little of the continent. Poor Clive has gone into Greece alone. How it pained me to leave him. There was a possibility of Herbert's joining him at Zante, but there is a report here that the Prince of Butera died suddenly, and that he was on the point of marrying the princess.[1]

5 *o'clock.*—Orlando is just arrived, and it has done me much good to see him. This is foreign post day, and the bell is going, I cannot, therefore, add a word more, but will write fully soon.

God bless you, my dear parents, &c., &c., &c.

---

[1] They were married 17th August, 1814.

CHISWICK PRESS :—PRINTED BY WHITTINGHAM AND WILKINS,
TOOKS COURT, CHANCERY LANE.